I0691405

Uniforms & Cumsluts

A collection of erotic gay stories

First Edition

Published by The Nazca Plains Corporation
Las Vegas, Nevada
2009

ISBN: 978-1-935509-26-4

Published by

The Nazca Plains Corporation ®
4640 Paradise Rd, Suite 141
Las Vegas NV 89109-8000

© 2009 by The Nazca Plains Corporation. All rights reserved.
No part of this work may be reproduced or utilized in any form or by any means, electronic or mechanical, including photocopying, microfilm, and recording, or by any information storage and retrieval system, without permission in writing from the publisher. Printed in the United States of America.

PUBLISHER'S NOTE
Uniforms & Cumsluts is a work of fiction created wholly by *Ted Gay*'s imagination. All characters are fictional and any resemblance to any persons living or deceased is purely by accident. No portion of this book reflects any real person or events.

Cover Photo, VishStudio
Art Director, Blake Stephens

DEDICATION

To my deceased life-partner's alter-ego who had erotic S&M stories published in a British gay magazine in the 1980s/1990s.

AUTHOR'S NOTE

These fictional stories sometimes include scenes of unprotected anal intercourse. In this day and age this is not a thing to be encouraged. These stories are pure fantasy, and some of the stories relate to the pre-HIV/ AIDS era. Even then, however, condoms would have protected us from many other STDs.

Uniforms & Cumsluts

A collection of erotic gay stories

First Edition

Ted Gay

CONTENTS

SERVICING THE USMC

Karl read the advert in the gay press with disbelief: 'Faggots needed to service the military. Applicants must be willing at all times to obey orders, and provide all orifices for military sexual use and abuse. No pay, accommodation will be in military cellblocks, cum-contaminated food and drink provided.'

Karl's heart missed several beats. He had always had a fetish for men in uniform, and this was just too good an opportunity to miss.

He sent off an email to the address given in the advert, and immediately came back a short, crisp instruction to report to USMC barracks in the city at 10.00 a.m. on the Saturday morning.

Two days away. Karl hardly slept the next two nights, and was up bright and early on the Saturday. He had a quick breakfast and headed off for the USMC barracks near the city center.

He showed the printout of the email summonsing him to the barracks at the main gate, and the smart, blond, handsome young marine on duty gave a smirk, came closer to the open car window and unzipped his flies.

1

Karl swallowed all the marine's orgasm, then crawled from under the desk as the marine zipped up his pants.

'You'll do fine here, but we need to break-in your ass and see if that gives as good service as your mouth. Thru that door, motherfucker!'

The marine indicated a door to his left marked 'Assbreaking'. Karl walked thru, and was immediately grabbed by two marines who frog-marched him into a room and strapped him face down on to a leather table marked 'Rape Bench'. They pulled his pants down, then one marine climbed on top of him, lubed up his ass and brutally stuck his big hard cock right in causing Karl to scream with pain. His scream was cut short as the other marine opened his flies and shoved his 12" monster cock into Karl's open mouth, stifling the scream.

'Shut the fuck up, cunt!' said the marine raping his ass. 'Lieutenant Creamer is feeding you some more breakfast while I break-in your ass for 1,000 marines. You're about to drink the biggest load you've ever tasted, queer boy! A real man's load!'

'How d'ya like Sergeant Assbreaker breaking you in for the barracks? 1,000 marines are going to be using your ass and mouth today, and every day. You'll be drinking so much marine cum you'll get drunk on it. We'll turn you into a marine jism junkie by the end of today, and your ass will just itch for a big marine's cock up it 24 hours a day,' said Lieut. Creamer, still fucking my mouth.

'Oh shit, I'm fuckin' cummin' up the faggot's ass!' screamed Sgt Assbreaker, as he pumped his load into me. I could feel his cock pumping out its juice. Sgt Assbreaker pulled out, and showed Lieut. Creamer and me his still stiff cock encased in a condom almost bursting with thick marine sperm.

'Oh God, the obscene sight of your orgasm's brought me off!' said Lieut. Creamer, as he closed his eyes in ecstasy and reached his climax inside my mouth. 'Now how do you like the flavor of THIS orgasm, boy?'

I swallowed the lieutenant's huge load - 20 spurts, which overflowed and dribbled down my chin.

'Your orgasm tastes delicious, Corporal Creamer, sir!' I replied as I licked some of it off my lips.

Sgt Assbreaker then scooped up the cum on my chin, and made me lick it off his fingers: 'Lieut. Creamer's fed you his orgasm, don't waste any of it, you ungrateful bitch,' he said.

Then I noticed Sgt Assbreaker was removing the cum-filled condom from his own cock, and was squeezing the contents on to a couple of cookies on a plate which Lieut. Creamer was holding.

'Finish your breakfast, and eat these cum cookies' said Lieut. Creamer. I picked up the cum-covered cookies and ate them ravenously.

'Did my cum taste good?' asked Sgt Assbreaker. 'Which orgasm tasted best?'

I didn't know what to reply, but they handed me a form to fill in. I had to describe in minute detail the flavor and consistency of all the marine cum I had eaten since I came on the base an hour ago. For each load I ate, I had to check a box to say whether it was creamy, runny, thick, sweet, bitter, etc.

At the end I had to say which load I preferred. I wrote, truthfully, that all USMC cum was delicious, and I'd be eager to drink any they offered me.

That was the right answer, as this was a test paper, and had I said one was better than the other, I'd have been rejected and lost the unpaid position of Faggot Servicer to the USMC in the city.

I had passed the first test, the next one was being gang-banged orally and anally by all 1,000 marines on the base. This went on all day, till my ass and mouth were sore. All the marines wore condoms when fucking my ass, and all the cum inside them was squeezed out over food and fed to me. Not one drop of marine cum was wasted.

By the end of the day I was like a limp rag doll, fucked to death. The erotic clean soapy smell of all those sexy young marines filled my nostrils, as did the taste of their sweet sperm. I was in heaven. These were clean, all-American fighting men, and I was privileged to be servicing them.

As a special end-of-day treat to all faggots who service the military well, I was allowed one privilege at the end of the day. Before retiring to my cell, I was taken into the FM Room, which I learnt stood for 'Faggot

Milking Room'. I was strapped naked to a crucifix-type device, and two young marines in full uniform fondled my balls, pulled my nipples, spat in my face, yelled obscenities at me, and took turns to jerk me off.

'Milk the fuckin' cow dry!' said the marine tweaking my nipples as the other one jerked my cock with a hand covered in baby oil. I was in ecstasy, but to make sure I shot a big load several marines first ejaculated into a champagne glass, filling it to the top with their sperm. This was then fed to me by one marine as the other jerked me off with his oily hands and expert fingers. They did indeed milk me dry. As I drank the cocktail of hot cum from the glass, the marine's expert milking fingers made me ejaculate a huge orgasm.

'OK, now you'll sleep well and be fit to service more marines tomorrow' said the marine who had just fed me the glass of sperm.

I was shown my cell, with just a straw mattress, a bucket for a toilet, and a stone hand basin. I fell exhausted on to the mattress and slept immediately, reliving the sexual abuse of the marines in my dreams.

I awoke to find a sweet-scented 18-year old marine cadet with flaming red hair straddling my neck and ordering me to open my fuckin' mouth, it was breakfast time. Five minutes later he fed me my first load of marine cum of the day, and it was the sweetest, most delicious load I'd tasted in my life. What a lovely way to be woken up!

ARMY PROPERTY

This is a fictional fantasy involving the British and U.S. military and civilians in imaginary and extreme S&M type sex and humiliation scenarios. It does not imply this sort of behavior is to be condoned, outside of voluntary role play by consenting adults.

I was 18 years old and on a peace demonstration at a military base in East Anglia, England. We had come equipped with ladders and mattresses in order to climb the boundary fences and safely scale the coiled barbed wire at the top.

About 20 of us from my group managed to scale the perimeter fence, and once inside we headed for the nearest military equipment we could locate armed with mallets, etc. to smash it to pieces. Some women made for an aircraft, climbed up on it and smashed the cockpit windows before climbing inside and smashing up the controls.

I somehow got separated from the others, and decided I'd head for a light armored vehicle and see what damage I could do to that.

Suddenly I tripped and fell flat on my face. As I tried to scramble up, I felt a boot in my back pressing me down into the ground again. Then I saw another pair of boots in front of my face; army boots beneath khaki trousers.

'OK, we've got another one,' said a voice above me, 'Let's take him to the interrogation hut'.

'Up you get, son,' said the soldier in front of me, as the boot was removed from my back.

Two British Army Military Policemen helped me to my feet, confiscated my sack with my mallet and tools, and escorted me towards a Nissan hut. They were dressed in their MP uniform of light khaki trousers and short-sleeved shirts, with red armbands and the letters MP written on them. On their short-cropped heads they wore the flat Redcap of the British Military Police.

I was taken into the hut, which was empty apart from a desk and some chairs. Pushing me down in a chair, one MP sat beside me whilst the other one faced me from behind the desk. The one next to me had red hair, and the one behind the desk was blond. Neither one could have been more than 25, and they were very good-looking indeed.

'OK, you anarchists have caused enough trouble on this base today.

We're gonna teach you a lesson,' snarled the one behind the desk.

'I'm not an anarchist', I said, 'I'm a peace protestor.'

'Why did you trespass on this base, and why come armed with these tools?' said the MP, pointing to the mallet and other tools on the desk, which he had confiscated from me.

'To smash up as much of your murderous equipment as I could,' I said. 'And I wasn't trespassing - my taxes pay for this base, and your wages. I'm carrying out an inspection on behalf of the British taxpayers, and destroying illegal equipment.'

'Insolent little bastard, isn't he?' said the soldier sitting next to me, 'I think we'll have to teach him to respect the British Army.'

'Yes, I think we will,' said the other soldier. 'Stand up! Get behind him, soldier, and show him the power of a British Military Policeman!'

The soldier next to me pulled me to my feet, and before I could protest he stood behind me with one arm round in front of my face, while the other made a grab for my crotch area. I could hardly breathe because the MP's bulging tattooed bicep was smothering my mouth and nose. I smelt a strong smell of soap, which was a tremendous sexual turn on, and at the same time his other hand was groping my cock which had quickly become rock hard inside my jeans.

'He's got a boner,' said the soldier behind me, 'We're gonna have some fun with this one. Read that tattoo on my arm,' he ordered me.

He flexed his bicep as he pulled it a few inches from my face so I could read what the tattoo said. 'OK, read it out loud,' he ordered in my ear.

'It…it says, B…Br… British Army S…Sp…Spunk…' I stammered.

'British Army Spunk, that's right! That's what you're up against. Now show respect for the British Army - lick that tattoo, go on, lick my bicep!' he ordered, still groping my cock inside my jeans, which was now leaking pre-cum.

I put out my tongue and did as he ordered, licking all over his tattoo and his muscular upper arm protruding from his khaki shirt and red MP armband. This made me so hot I almost came in my pants. Meanwhile, the other Military Policeman came round from behind the desk and stood in front of me.

'Sit him down on the chair again,' he ordered, and the other soldier pushed me down into the chair, pulling his own chair up close to mine. He unzipped my jeans, and took my stiff cock out. 'Look here, Corporal. He's got a raging erection.'

'Yes, he's a bloody queer. We know why he really came on to this base, to get near to soldiers. He is hoping we will rape him and sexually abuse him. Well, it's your lucky day, son,' said the soldier standing in front of me, unzipping his khaki trousers and waving his long, smooth, circumcised cock in my face. 'Have you ever sucked a soldier's cock before? Ever been orally raped by a Military Policeman, son? Well open your fuckin' mouth 'cos I'm gonna feed you some of that British Army Spunk you just read about on Private Richardson's arm.'

'Open your mouth for Corporal Williams,' said Pvte Richardson in my ear, now wanking my cock with one hand and forcing my mouth open with the other. Not that it needed much forcing, I secretly knew they were absolutely right. I did want to be raped and sexually abused not by just these two, but by all the British and American male soldiers on the camp, or at least those under the age of about 30 anyway. I opened my mouth, and Corporal Williams' sweet smelling cock forced its way right in, spewing his even sweeter tasting pre-cum all over my tongue.

'Yes, you like the taste of Corporal Williams' cock, don't you son,' cooed Pvte Richardson obscenely in my ear, whist spitting in his hand and slowly lubricating the tip of my cock with his spit-covered hand. 'Suck the Corporal's cock, that's right, suck it hard and he'll feed you your lunch.'

By now I was in a frenzy of spunk-lust for these two soldiers. All resistance to the military had ebbed away, all I wanted to do at this moment was to serve them and do whatever they wanted. They sensed this, for Corporal Williams sneered: 'He's not so cocky now, is he? Wait till you get a bellyful of our spunk inside you, that will quell any rebellious tendencies you still harbor against the British Army. Now look into my fuckin' face when I'm talking to you, that's right - keep looking while I feed you your first meal of soldier sperm. And not just soldier sperm, you're getting the creme de la creme, Military Policeman's cum!'

'Look into Corporal Williams' face,' said Pvte Richardson. 'See, it's contorted with lust, son! That means he's near to his climax. Look into his eyes - look, they're glazing over with sheer lust as he reaches his orgasm. He's feeding you hot soldier spunk, son. Feel that

Military Police cock spurting Army cream into your mouth. Yes, your mouth's filling up with soldier's sperm. Taste it, do you like the sweet taste of Corporal Williams' orgasm?'

I nodded: 'Yes' as my mouth was flooded with the most delicious cum I have ever tasted, and I had to keep swallowing as the soldier filled my mouth again and again. I thought he would never stop cumming. I almost came myself, but Pvte Richardson sensed this and stopped massaging the tip of my cock.

'That's right, drink down your lunch while it's still hot,' said Pvte Richardson, 'Then I'll feed you my hot load'.

He stood up and as Corporal Williams at last stopped shooting his load and removed his cock from my mouth, Pvte Richardson unzipped his fly and replaced Williams' cock with his own. I sucked on it like a baby at its mother's breast - I wanted more of this delicious British Military Policeman spunk. Now Corporal Williams sat in the chair next to me and was jerking me off as I sucked Private Richardson's big cock.

'Yes, you are hooked on British Army semen now, aren't you my little beauty,' he said in my ear. 'Keep sucking, he's about to feed you your second helping of soldier cum.'

Corporal Williams was jerking me faster and faster, as Private Williams fucked my mouth. His big cock went right down my throat, causing me to gag.

'That's right, choke on his cock, you bastard', said Corporal Williams in my ear. 'We've killed people like that, you know - choked them to death with our big soldier cocks! Some just drowned in our spunk - they couldn't cope with 500 soldiers spunking down their throats one after the other. That's gonna happen to you on this base, son. This is just the beginning, so get used to swallowing soldier cum or you'll drown or choke to death!'

I was now close to cumming, and so was Private Richardson, I could tell by the look of ecstasy on his face, the stiffening of his cock in my

mouth, and the fact that his eyes were now half-closed as he reached his climax.

'That's right, shoot your load, son. Show us how much you are enjoying your lunch of soldier sperm. Drink that Military Police spunk!' said Corporal Williams as he brought me to climax. 'That's right, shoot, son, shoot that load'

I shot all over Private Richardson's trousers just as he started shooting his hot load into my mouth and down my throat: 'Did you enjoy that orgasm?' asked Private Richardson, 'Then taste this one!' and my mouth was working overtime swallowing mouthful after mouthful of his sperm, which had a different flavor from Corporal Williams' but which was just as delicious.

As Private Richardson removed his cock from my mouth, I sank back into my chair exhausted and happy, but they weren't finished with me yet.

'You've been fed lunch, but you must be thirsty,' said Corporal Richardson, 'Would you like something hot to drink?'

'Oh, yes please,' I said, thinking they were going to make a pot of tea. Instead they both stood in front of me and told me to open my mouth wide again. A moment later they were both urinating in my mouth!

'Fuckin' drink soldier piss,' said Corporal Williams. 'Keep swallowing, your mouth's gonna be used as an Army latrine for this base! Thousands of soldiers are gonna use your mouth, son!'

'That's right, stop spilling your hot piss cocktail!' barked Private Williams, 'Swallow! Swallow these nice hot drinks Corporal Williams and I are giving you, you ungrateful little bastard!'

I gulped down as much of the foul tasting liquid as I could, but still got soaked in their piss. However, I found the more I swallowed, the more I got used to the taste. It was actually turning me on again, to be forced to drink piss from the cocks of these two handsome young military policemen. After a few seconds I had taken both their pissing

cocks inside my mouth and was swallowing nearly all their piss. My belly was filling up with it.

Afterwards I felt disgusted with myself, and tried to protest: 'That was disgusting! I can't be treated like that, I know my rights!'

Corporal Williams and Private Richardson grabbed hold of me and both of them gobbed and spat right in my face and into my mouth. 'Rights? You ain't got any fuckin' rights here, son!' yelled Corporal Williams.

'No, you're just Army Property now, to do as we like with,' said Private Richardson.

They then made clear what lay in store for me in the days and weeks ahead. I was to be kept prisoner indefinitely on the base.

'Tomorrow you're on latrine duty for the British soldiers,' said Private Richardson.

'And when our lads have finished using your mouth as a latrine and a cum-dump, we'll hand you over to our horny American friends. Have you ever been raped by 5,000 sex-mad U.S. Marines, son?' laughed Corporal Williams.

They walked off laughing, and locked the door of the hut behind me. I had to sleep on the hard floor, but dreamt of fellatio and anal rape, and of being used as a latrine by thousands of British and American soldiers and marines. This was to become reality in the weeks, months and years which lay ahead. I was now Army Property.

Later that evening the Army tattooist came into the hut. He took out his equipment, and whilst two soldiers held me down he tattooed something on my forehead. It was painful, but my pain was eased by the two soldiers wanking me as the tattooing took place. Between them the two young soldiers brought me off, just as the tattooist finished. They then held up two mirrors so I could see what the tattoo was.

In the first mirror I could only see words written backwards across my forehead, but when I looked at the second mirror in the first I could

read the words: 'BRITISH ARMY & USMC PROPERTY'. Worse still, across my upper lip, just below my nose had been tattooed the word : 'SOLDIERS" and below my bottom lip the word 'URINAL'. I now knew I'd never be set free, couldn't be set free. I could never go home to my friends and family, couldn't face anyone looking like this. I was indeed Army Property, and everyone could see what my mouth was to be used for.

Later that evening, after the tattooist had been, one of his assistants came in with two soldiers. The soldiers held me down in the chair whilst the tattooist's assistant got some evil looking tools out of a case he carried with him.

'What are you going to do?' I asked. Hadn't I been thru enough indignities already?

'You fuckin' know what is tattooed on your forehead,' said one of the soldiers. 'We can't risk losing any of our army property. So we're gonna pierce your pussy-boy tits and put a chain on 'em. You won't be going far when we chain you up by your nipples, lad.'

Some more soldiers came into the hut, carrying a wooden piece of equipment. As they set it up next to my chair I realized what it was - a pair of stocks like they had in medieval times. They made me bend over and put my head and hands into three cut-away sections, then they closed and padlocked the top, so I was bent over with my head and hands locked thru three holes in the crossbar. One soldier then moved around the front, unzipped his fly and waved his big cock in my face.

'Open up, son, you must be hungry by now. Time for your supper!' he said. Just at that moment I felt another soldier pulling down my trousers, and then he started lubricating my arse. 'I said open your fuckin' mouth,' said the first soldier, hitting me hard on the cheek. The impact made me instantly open my mouth wide, and he shoved his 8" of solid man-meat right in and down my throat.

'You're gonna be raped at both ends, son,' said the other soldier, as he started fingering my bumhole. 'We're gonna break you in for the whole fuckin' camp! Not that he's a virgin, I bet this little faggot has taken a load of fuckin' cocks in every hole in his pussy-boy body!'

'Yeah, he's got a lovely wet cunt mouth,' said the first soldier. 'It feels just like my girlfriend's wet pussy. And don't you dare bite me or I'll knock all your fuckin' teeth, out. Just accept my cock and you'll soon be rewarded with some fuck-juice for your supper!'

As I tried not to gag on his cock, the other soldier started entering my back passage. His cock was massive - so thick it really hurt me as it went in. I tried to scream, but with the other cock in my mouth all I did was bite on it. Instantly the first soldier punched me on the nose. 'No fuckin' teeth! I won't warn you again, son!'

'He's not used to taking real men's cocks. He's just taken faggot tools before,' said the soldier behind me, who had now worked his thick prick right into my hole. Still it was going in further, stretching my hole till I thought it would be ripped apart. He certainly was a real man - he voiced what I was thinking at that moment: 'That's right, son, you're being raped by two strapping soldiers! And you better get used to it, because this is your life from now on. We're short of good pussy on this base. All the women soldiers are fuckin' lesbians with faces like the back of a bus, or else they look like fuckin' men. You are the prettiest thing we've seen round here for a long time. He's got a cute little arse - it's gonna turn the whole fuckin' camp on, shaggin' this little beauty of a pussy!'

As the two soldiers fucked me from both ends, the other soldiers who'd brought the stocks in stood and watched, jerking their cocks, whilst the tattooist's assistant crawled under me and started to work on my nipples. The pain was excruciating as he pierced my tender nipples, and the huge cock in my backside was painful too as it seemed to tear me apart. But I got no mercy, the two soldiers fucked me from both ends till they were ready to cum.

'I'm fuckin' cummin' dahn his throat,' said the first soldier as his cock started pumping hot sperm right down my gullet. I had to keep swallowing to keep from gagging.

'Yeah, and I'm gonna cream up his shit-hole, here it is, pussy-boy!' said the other soldier as his massive cock started filling my arse up with soldier cream. As the first soldier finally removed his cock from my mouth, I shouted to the soldier behind me: 'You didn't even use a condom!'

15

chair in front of me and squeezed out the spunky contents of the used condom on to the biscuit.

'There you are, son - a nice piece of shortbread covered in my sperm for you to eat', he said, picking up the spunk-covered biscuit and forcing me to eat it. The soldiers all laughed as I chewed and swallowed, whilst the tattooist's assistant was attaching a metal ring thru each of my newly-pierced nipples, and on to these rings he then attached a long metal chain. The soldiers then fitted a leather collar with iron spikes around my neck. This also had a chain attached. Finally they attached a sort of leather harness around my cock and balls, and this also had a chain attached. They then undid the stocks, and the soldiers led me across the hut - one pulling my neck chain, one my cock chain, and two had hold of the chain attached to my nipples. I had to keep up or it hurt me where the chains pulled, especially the one on my nipples.

Whilst I had been operated on and raped in the stocks, some soldiers had dumped a load of hay and straw in one corner of the hut.

'There's your bed, dogboy!' shouted one of the soldiers. 'And these are for a drink and some food in case you get hungry.' He showed me two empty dog bowls on the floor marked 'Fido'. 'We'll fill them up later, and here's your toilet,' he said, throwing a rusty old bucket at the stack of hay.

I sat down on the pile of hay as the soldiers left, and presently more soldiers came in. One had a tin of dog food, which he emptied into one of the bowls. There were six soldiers, and all of them then jerked off over the dog food, till it was covered in their spunk. They then all pissed in the empty dog bowl till it was overflowing with their piss.

'Goodnight, dogboy! And make sure those two bowls are empty in the morning. We've got a video camera on you - you're gonna be in S&M porn movies, son! So don't even think of chucking the food and piss in that bucket, or we'll make you eat and drink the entire contents of that as well!'

With that they left and locked the door. I was tired out from all the shagging I had received, but I looked longingly at the food they had left me. It did look delicious. What was I thinking - delicious? I was a human being, and this was contaminated dog food - dog food covered in the spunk of six soldiers! I didn't care, I crawled over to the bowl and smelt

it - the spunky smell had my cock hard again. Like a good doggy, I stuck out my tongue and tasted the soldier cum - lovely! I'd really gotten a taste for it. It wasn't long before I'd lapped up all the spunky dog meat in the bowl, then I crawled over to the other bowl full of the piss of six soldiers. I smelt it, and again the odor was delicious. I lapped it all up, laid back on the hay and jerked myself off. Satisfied and happy in my new slave-role, I fell asleep, wondering what lay in store for me in the morning.

I should have known. 6 a.m. I was woken by Reveille - a bugler came right into my hut and blasted the wake-up call in my ear. Then he bawled at me: 'Wakey wakey! Rise and shine! You're in the army now, get out on the fuckin' parade ground! 2,000 soldiers are waiting to be serviced! I hope you're hungry, 'cos you're gonna get the biggest breakfast you ever had!'

I was directed to a tap in the corner of the hut where I had to wash and shave in cold water, then I had to quickly dress and was led out of the hut by three soldiers pulling me by my nipple, cock and neck chains. They took me across the army camp to the parade ground. I could see lines of soldiers in smart uniforms already lined up. As we got nearer, I could see they all had their flies open and their big cocks out. They were jerking them to make them hard. There really must have been 2,000 soldiers in ranks - how on Earth was I expected to service that lot, I thought, even though my mouth watered at the thought of all that army spunk. It simply wasn't possible, it would take me too long.

We reached the parade ground, and the soldiers made me kneel down on a little trolley. They then handcuffed me to the sides of this trolley, and started to wheel me out to the first rank of soldiers, who by now all had their cocks stiff and hard poking out of their flies and waiting for my mouth to service them.

It was then I noticed some of my colleagues who had been on the peace protest the day before. They too were shackled up in chains and handcuffs and were being made to kneel on similar trolleys. Each male protestor had two ranks of soldiers to service.

'Yes, 19 of your anarchist friends are here too. They've been pacified with soldier spunk and made subservient to the army too. You're all army property now,' said one of the three soldiers maneuvering my trolley across the parade ground.

'And we haven't forgotten the women who smashed up that aircraft,' said one of the other soldiers, 'They are being taken care of in another part of the camp. The lesbian soldiers are having first go at them, and then the men will have their turn.'

'Right now, there's 100 soldier-boy cocks waiting for your mouth to service them,' said the third soldier. 'Two ranks of 50 soldiers - here we are at the first rank. Get your mouth open and ready, boy!'

They wheeled my trolley up to the first soldier in the first line on the parade ground. I found myself kneeling on my little trolley with a soldier in full uniform in front of me, standing to attention with his stiff, hard cock sticking out of his fly and also standing to attention.

As if to echo my thoughts, the commanding officer on his platform shouted out to the whole parade ground: 'AttenSHUN! Cocks ready for sucking off! OK men, start feeding the prisoners their breakfast now. First man in line, one pace forward NOW! Insert penis in prisoner's mouth NOW! Prisoners suck off soldier cocks NOW!'

The soldier in front of me stepped smartly forward, and still standing to attention shoved his big cock right down my throat. I nearly gagged, but knew I had to suck him off quickly if I didn't want to be beaten up by the three soldiers who were escorting me. Two of them knelt on my trolley beside me and started mouthing obscenities in my ears, whilst the third soldier kept pushing my head forward on to the cock in my mouth.

'Suck that soldier's cock,' said a voice in my right ear. 'That's right, suck it hard. Remember the smell and taste of his cock. This is Private Jay Smith. By next week you must learn to recognize him and all the other 100 soldiers you will be servicing today by their smell and taste.'

'That's right,' said the soldier's voice in my left ear. 'Next week you'll be blindfolded, and you'll have to name correctly every soldier by the smell and taste of his cock and spunk. So when he shoots in your mouth in a few moments, keep his cum in your mouth until you remember the flavor.'

'Ready to feed prisoner, SIR!' shouted the soldier in front of me, as his cock stiffened in my mouth and I felt his cock head swelling up ready to spurt his load. 'Cummin' in his mouth now, SIR!'

As he said that a huge jet of thick, hot soldier cum shot out of his cock on to my tongue. It tasted sweet, but with a touch of spice. The first spurt was followed quickly by five more, which I held in my mouth as long as I could, but I had to start swallowing as more soldier spunk was pumped into my already full mouth.

'Remember the taste of that cum - that's Private Jay Smith's orgasm you're tasting, son,' said the voice in my right ear. 'Look up at his face, and see who's just fed you your first helping of spunk today.'

As the soldier took his cock out of my mouth and took one pace backwards into line, I looked up and saw his face for the first time. He was about my age - 18, with blue eyes and short cropped blond hair visible beneath his peaked army cap.

'Where are your manners, boy! Thank Private Smith for feeding you his sperm,' said the soldier on my left, slapping me in the face.

Still looking up at the handsome young soldier who had just fed me, I said: 'Thank you, sir, for feeding me your cum.'

The young soldier looked down at me as if I was a piece of dog-shit he had just spotted on the parade-ground. He spat in my face and sneered: 'That's not all I'll be feeding you before the day's out, fuck-face!' We may have been about the same age, but I was definitely his inferior.

'OK, service the next soldier in line,' said the soldier to my right as they pushed my trolley along to the next guardsman. 'There's a nice big soldier cock for you to suck on - think of all the soldier spunk that will pump down your throat,' he said.

The soldier must have had a 10" cock, and as he suddenly took one pace forward the monster dong hit me smack in the face, smothering it with the guardsman's gooey pre-cum.

'Don't he look pretty with soldier cock juice all over his face,' said the soldier on my left, 'Now open your fuckin' mouth and let him fuck it. This nice soldier wants to feed you hot cum straight from his big cock. Isn't that kind of him? Aren't you excited? How do you like being orally raped by 100 soldiers on the parade ground, boy? Get that cock down your

throat - this soldier needs to feel your warm, wet pussy-cunt of a mouth draining him dry of his baby-juice!'

I opened my mouth as wide as I could to accommodate the soldier's massive weapon. He rammed it right down my throat, and I almost choked. But I remembered I had to relax or I might choke to death.

'That's right,' said the soldier to my right, 'Submit and take it all down your throat. See those 10 medals on this guardsman's chest?' I glanced up and saw 10 phallus-shaped medals on his tunic. 'That means this big soldier has choked 7 civilians to death by orally raping them, and 3 more choked to death on his cum, so you better swallow quick when he shoots. Remember the smell and flavor of his cock and spunk though, you've got to identify him blindfolded when you suck him off next week!'

I had already fixed in my mind how to identify the first soldier I had sucked off today - sweet and spicy spunk, that was Pvte Jay Smith. I didn't think I'd have much trouble identifying this cock blindfold, it was so big. But I knew I couldn't afford to make a mistake, or I'd be punished. His cock had been lubricated with something which was slimy and tasted of peppermint. The soldier I was sucking off spoke to me: 'Like the minty taste, son? I covered my cock with a special treat so you'd enjoy your breakfast more. Remember that minty taste, boy! When you taste that, you're sucking off the biggest cock in the camp - Private Robin Wexford. How d'ya like me fuckin' your throat, son?'

I nodded as best I could, as I struggled with the massive tool rammed down my throat, fucking it like a woman's cunt. I felt the monster prick stiffen as it prepared to shoot its huge load down my throat. Seconds later the soldier was moaning in ecstasy as he shot pints of thick, hot, spunky fluid straight down my throat, bypassing my tongue. I knew this was no good - I had to get a taste of his load just in case I didn't recognize his cock next week. I pulled my mouth away a little, so the next six jets of spunk went right into my mouth and coated my tongue. He was gushing soldier cum like a geyser, I had to swallow quickly or I would indeed have choked to death on his massive load. His cum tasted slightly bitter, with a hint of almonds. I'd remember when blindfolded that this bitter almond flavored cum from the minty monster cock was the intimate very personal essence of Pvte Robin Wexford. I drank in his big manly soldier smell. I loved him, worshiped him, and I hadn't even seen his face yet!

The obscenity of what I and my colleagues were doing suddenly hit me. We were sucking off ranks of soldiers, one after the other, on the parade ground of this army camp, in front of their officers. I couldn't believe the depravity of what the Army was doing to peaceful civilian protestors. I didn't have much more time for such thoughts, as I was ordered to look up at the soldier I'd just sucked off and thank him for my meal.

'Did you enjoy eating that filthy mess?' asked the soldier, who I could now see was over 6ft tall, with a muscular body and a face which reminded me of Matt Damon. Very sexy indeed. I did love him, he was my favorite on the camp so far!

'Oh yes, sir! Thank you so much for letting me swallow your delicious orgasm, sir! I love you, sir!' I said.

He saluted and said: 'For Queen and Country! A soldier's always ready to shoot! My weapon's always primed and ready to fire, boy!'

As I was pushed along to the next soldier in line, I could see all the soldiers were now jerking their cocks. The soldier behind me pushing the trolley saw me looking, and said: 'Yes, they're getting primed ready to shoot straight in your mouth, boy! We haven't got all day, you'll just have a few seconds to swallow each soldier's load then on to the next one. But remember the taste of each one.'

So we moved on down the line. It went like this: I was wheeled to the next soldier, he stepped forward and spunked into my mouth and the soldiers pushing my trolley took it in turns to say each soldier's name.

I then had to thank the soldier for my cummy meal, and it was on to the next.

Down the line I went: 'Drink my spunky load, son.' 'Did you enjoy Private Derek Young's cum load, boy?' Sweet and thick, with globs of jelly-like spunk, I memorized the consistency. 'Thank you, sir!' 'Next! Private John Wilkins'... etc., etc.

I was getting so many soldier spunk loads in my mouth, all a different flavor and consistency. How would I remember them all? I had to associate their name with something in the unique flavor and smell of their cocks and cum. I only had a week to learn it all. This was so utterly depraved, I could hardly believe it was happening.

'By the way,' said one of the soldiers pushing my trolley as we got to the end of the first rank of soldiers, and started working our way back along the second rank, 'Once you've memorized all these soldiers' loads, and can recognize them blindfolded from the taste of their spunk, you and your pals will be moved to the next two ranks. In the next few weeks you'll all have serviced the 2,000 soldiers on this parade ground, and memorized all their names from the taste of their loads in your mouths! You won't be allowed to recognize them by their faces, only by the flavor and consistency of their spunk in your mouth. This is so you can thank them by name when they feed you thru the glory hole of the suck-off cubicle where you'll be imprisoned for the rest of your useful life. The only time you'll be let out is to service new recruits, who you'll also have to memorize by their unique spunk taste.'

I couldn't believe what I was hearing. I was going to be locked up in a cubicle, with just a glory hole to feed me soldier spunk, and presumably piss, from anonymous soldier cocks. I wouldn't ever see their faces (except for the new recruits), just have to recognize them from the taste of their loads and the smell of their cocks.

'Disgusting, isn't it?' said the soldier to my right, as I sucked off another soldier's cock. 'Bet you didn't think the Army did this sort of thing to civilians. We're trained to kill, boy - just you remember that! You and your anarchist peacenik friends are lucky we prefer to have fun by using you as fuck-meat!'

'Yes sir, thank you sir!', I said as I swallowed my 52nd load of cum this morning. Thin and watery - Private Jim Collins, I made a mental note as we moved to the 53rd soldier.

'If you think this is disgusting and depraved, wait till this afternoon,' laughed the soldier to my left. 'Remember, it's latrine duty for you and your pacifist mates this afternoon. I hope you're all thirsty for soldiers' stinking hot urine!'

I kept on swallowing soldier spunk until we finally got to the last soldier in the second line. As I got my 100th mouthful of army cum I found it hard to swallow it - all the soldier sperm had filled my belly and seemed to be stuck in my throat. No matter how hard I swallowed the last few loads wouldn't go down - I was literally full up. 'Private Jason Clark' said the soldier to my right, as I tried to remember the flavor of his

cum. 'Thank you, sir. Thank you for feeding me your sweet sperm, sir!' I said.

'Look at his belly, it's bulging obscenely with soldier spunk! He looks like a pregnant woman,' laughed the soldier on my right as they wheeled me and my colleagues back to our respective huts for a rest before going on latrine duty, whatever that meant.

'Yes, and it's oozing out of his mouth and nostrils too - and he's got soldiers' cum all over his face! It's disgusting! Sheer fuckin' filth!' said the soldier on my left, whilst the third soldier was taking pictures.

'Bet your parents would love to see these,' said the soldier taking the pictures. 'If ever you try to escape, we'll make sure they get the videos and pictures we've taken of you this morning and yesterday, and the ones we'll take in the latrine this afternoon of you drinking pints of army piss.'

'I won't try to escape,' I promised. 'I love it here. You are all so kind to me, thank you so very much for feeding me such delicious army food and for teaching me respect for the British Army'.

'Respect? You ain't learned nothin' yet, son!' said the soldier taking photos of my cum-covered face. 'Wait till you've been used as a soldier's urinal all afternoon, and gang-raped up the arse by a hundred soldiers. That'll teach you respect, boy!'

'And all that is just to break you in for the 5,000 American marines on the camp to use as their plaything', said one of the soldiers pushing my trolley.

We came to my hut, and they threw me in. Several of my colleagues were in there already.

'Right, this is prisoner hut number 3,' said one of the soldiers.

'You'll be kept together from now on. You'll all eat from the dog-bowls and use the buckets for your toilets.'

They then chained us all up around the walls, each with bundle of hay to sleep on, two dog bowls filled with spunk-covered dog food and soldier piss, and a rusty bucket to piss and shit in. We couldn't move far with

the chains attached to our neck collars, just up and down like dogs on a leash. We couldn't reach each other. It was embarrassing, having to eat cum-covered dog food and drink soldier piss from the dog bowls in front of some of my best friends. What made it worse, I suddenly spotted my elder brother over in the far corner. So he had been captured too. He tried to avoid making eye contact, and I was disgusted as I saw him lap up the soldier piss in his dog bowl. But what else could we do? We were given nothing else to drink, and we certainly couldn't reach the cold water tap in the corner because of the chains.

Then three soldiers walked in, and pointed to me and my brother.

'So you two are brothers, are you?' said one of the soldiers. 'We've just been thru the prisoners' papers, and we see you have the same surname and address. Bet mum and dad are wondering where there precious boys are, if only they could see you now.'

'OK, we're gonna have some more fun,' said the second soldier, as he came over and unchained me from the wall. He led me over to my elder brother, who was aged 20. I had always secretly fancied him, but being brothers we'd never done anything sexual together. Besides he was straight, with a girlfriend. At least he WAS straight till the Army captured us.

'On your knees and give your brother a nice slow blow-job,' ordered the soldier who had led me over to the corner where my brother stood.

The third soldier got my brother's smooth circumcised cock out of his trousers and started masturbating it to make it hard.

'Your little brother's going to suck you off and drink your load,' he said. 'And we're gonna film it all!'

One of the soldiers started the video camera, as I was pushed to my knees in front of my brother, and he was forced to enter my mouth.

'That's right, suck your brother's big cock. Do you like the smell and taste of his prick? Nice, isn't it? Suck out all his sweet hot cum, there's a good boy,' said the soldier kneeling beside me, who was now jerking me off.

`This is so wrong, it's filthy and incestuous. I don't want to do this,' said my brother, who was a Christian and quite religious. But the army could corrupt anyone.

The third soldier standing behind my brother shoved some poppers up his nose.

'Oh, but you DO want to do this! You've wanted to fuck you little brother's mouth and arse for years, admit it!' said the soldier.

As the poppers took effect, breaking down his inhibitions, my brother started moaning as he fucked my mouth: 'Oh Jesus forgive me! Yeah, yeah - I've always wanted to fuck your little girly mouth and arse!' I couldn't believe my brother was saying these things to me, what was the Army doing to us? 'Drink my spunk, you know you've always wanted to. That's right, drink your big brother's spunky load, swallow it all down!'

'Another Christian corrupted', said one of the soldiers, rubbing his hands in glee. 'And we've got it all on videotape, him feeding his little brother!'

My brother shot his load in my mouth, and it was absolutely delicious! I felt utterly depraved as I swallowed it, but worse was to follow. Or rather better was to follow, I was now so confused as to what was right and what was wrong.

'I think your brother needs to piss now,' said the soldier who was jerking me off.

'Yes, your little brother is thirsty - give him a hot drink of your piss,' said the soldier taking the video.

The soldier behind my brother shoved the poppers up his nose again. After a few seconds hesitation he succumbed, and said: `D'ya wanna drink your big brother's piss? Open your mouth then, here it comes! Enjoy, you dirty little fucker!'

The soldier next to me wanked me right off as my brother started pissing in my mouth, and all over me. I was drenched in his piss, and I swallowed loads of it.

The soldier jerking me off whispered in my ear: 'Yeah, drink your brother's hot piss. You love the strong flavor, don't you? This is just a taste of what you'll get from the soldiers when you're on latrine duty this afternoon.'

I shot my load, as my brother continued to fill my mouth and throat with his piss.

'OK, back to your place. We'll make sure your brother fucks your arse and mouth every day,' said the soldier, leading me back and chaining me to the wall again. 'Have a rest for a few hours. You're all on urinal duty in the main barrack latrines at 12 noon.'

I sat on the hay, and looked over at my brother. He tried to avoid my eyes, but eventually our eyes met. He sneered at me and shouted across the hut: 'You dirty little faggot piss-drinker! You got me into this mess. Persuading me to come on this peace demo. Now they're trying to turn me into a faggot like you!'

'I'm sorry,' I sniveled.

'Yeah, well from now on I'm gonna use your arse and mouth whenever I can,' said my brother. 'You are gonna be the lowest of the low. We may be sex slaves of the army, but you're gonna be my personal slave. A slave of your slave brother, you can't get lower than that! Cunt faced girly boy, I should've raped you years ago! You were begging for it.'

We sat around thinking of all the spunk we'd swallowed that morning from the soldiers on the parade ground, and wondered exactly what urinal duty in the latrines would mean. It didn't really take much imagination from what had already occurred. Oh God, I was EXCITED!

In the early afternoon soldiers came in to our hut, unchained us from the walls and marched us out to the barrack blocks. We were taken into the latrines, where a line of urinals were installed along one wall. In between each urinal basin had been placed a stool, and behind each stool were four metal rings set in the wall. Two were just above floor level, and two were higher. We were all made to sit on these stools, and our arms and ankles were shackled to the rings on the wall. The soldiers then showed us signs which were to be hung around our necks. They read: 'Urinals, all ranks for the use of' with an arrow pointing up towards our mouths.

Also on the walls behind us, above the sets of metal rings, were strange wooden contraptions. These were opened up and our heads were locked into them. They were sort of like the wooden stocks used earlier, only these were only for our heads. A block under our chins made out heads tilt backwards. Finally funnels were placed in our mouths with the words: 'Soldiers' Urinals' painted on the insides in large black letters. Because of the angle our heads were locked in, and the fact that our arms and legs were shackled to the wall, it was impossible for us to remove the funnels from our mouths.

'OK, I hope you're all thirsty, because all afternoon soldiers from these barracks are going to be coming in and using the urinals,' said the lance corporal in charge before the soldiers left us. 'The soldiers may, of course, use the permanent urinals next to you, but they may take pity on you and use your funnels so you get a nice hot drink. You have no control at all over the situation - remember you are just army property!'

The soldiers who had brought us here then left, and we sat and waited for our first customers. We didn't have to wait long. A tall soldier in uniform with short-cropped reddish hair came in, and made for the ceramic urinal next to me. Then suddenly he looked right into my eyes, spat in my face, and sidled over to me. Pointing his big cock straight into the funnel protruding from my mouth he started to piss into it saying: 'You look as if you need a long, hot drink. I've been saving this up since last night especially for you! Don't you dare spill a drop!'

His piss was dark and strong, and the flavor almost made me puke. But the funnel was quickly filling up with the steaming hot liquid, and I knew I had to swallow as fast as I could. For two whole minutes he emptied the contents of his bladder into the funnel in my mouth, and I just had to keep swallowing. Then he just zipped up and walked away.

More soldiers came in, all in full uniform. Not one of them used the ceramic urinals; they all took a perverse pleasure in using the funnels in our mouths, and in making humiliating comments about quenching our thirst or how much they liked the new urinals.

All afternoon soldiers came in and used our mouths as their toilets. We had been warned we mustn't piss ourselves, and tight leather sheaths had been fitted over our cocks to stop us. So our bellies swelled up with all the soldier piss we were forced to drink. I felt mine would burst, when six more soldiers came in.

28

One of them carried a bucket, which they placed in the middle of the floor. All six soldiers then stood around it and pissed in it. More soldiers came in and used the bucket, till it was full up.

'Who's gonna be the lucky one who gets to drink this soldier piss cocktail?' asked one of the soldiers. There were six of us chained to the wall between the ceramic urinals, so the soldiers wrote down the numbers 1-6 and put them in one of their caps. I was number 6, and sure enough when one of the soldiers picked a number out of the cap it was number 6.

They all came over to my funnel and removed it from my mouth. One of them then produced a hosepipe, and put one end of it into the bucket of steaming hot soldier piss. He put the other end in my mouth and ordered me to suck and keep sucking. I did as I was told, and presently a never ending stream of soldier urine from the bucket entered my mouth. There was no way of stopping it till the bucket was empty. My belly grew bigger and bigger, till I felt sure it would burst.

The soldiers stood around laughing, as I swallowed the cocktail of soldier piss from the bucket. When it was empty they removed the hose from my mouth, and the funnels from the mouths of the other captives. They then unchained us, and I had to be helped up from my stool as I was now so heavy and my stomach was aching from all the soldier piss in my belly. They then took us over to the ceramic urinals, and took the sheaths off our cocks.

'OK, you may now relieve yourselves,' they said, and I gradually felt some of the pain subside as I pissed for what seemed 20 minutes.

We were then led back to our hut and chained up again. We were told to rest for an hour or so, then we were to be taken to the American Marines' quarters so their new recruits could try us out.

My brother and I were unchained and taken out together. We were marched across the base to where an American flag was flying from a pole. A sign nearby said United States Marine Corps. My brother and I were taken into a building, where two U.S. marines in smart uniforms stood to attention either side of a desk. At the desk sat a U.S. Marine officer.

'These two are brothers, they broke into the base yesterday to cause trouble, but are now very willing to serve your boys in any way they can,' said the British soldiers who had brought us here.

'Brothers, are they?' said the American officer, who was smoking a huge cigar, 'Well Uncle Sam can certainly make use of them. For a start, they can relieve my guards here. Stand 'em in front of my boys, then you can leave. I'll do the rest!'

I was placed in front of the marine on his right. He was a young white lad, about 18. My brother was made to stand before the other marine, who was a very handsome mixed-race black boy about the same age. The British soldiers then left saying they'd be back later.

The Marine officer went over to the young marine facing my brother, and pointed to him.

'You are looking at a cadet of the United States Marine Corps,' he said. 'Take a good look - he's an All-American boy. Now take a step nearer, that's right get up real close like you would if you were in hand-to-hand combat and he was about to kill ya, boy! He could, he could kill you limey scum with his bare hands for breaking into our base. Yes OUR base. It may say British Army base outside, but that's bullshit! We run this base, we occupy this fuckin' country, we fuckin' rule the WORLD! Understand me, you limey shitheads?'

'Y...Y...Yes, s...s...sir!' my poor brother stammered, as he was made to stand right up close to the marine.

'Now smell him, that's right, I said fuckin' SMELL him!' shouted the officer, 'What do you smell? A good, clean, all-American boy, that's what! You smell your fuckin' rulers, your fuckin' occupiers, the American master race, that's what you're smelling boy! Now lick his neck, go on - lick that clean all-American neck - taste good, boy? That's because he's brought up in the best country in the world, raised to rule ungrateful shit like you!

Now move down to his arms - look at those arms, boy! They could kill you, he's been trained to kill in unarmed combat. He could break your fuckin' limey neck. Shall I order him to break your fuckin' neck, boy?'

'N...no! P...P...Please d...don't k...k...kill me, s...sir!' pleaded my brother.

'Well lick his arms, lick those strong biceps which could kill you. If you lick hard enough he might take pity on you and let you suck his fuckin' cock instead' said the officer.

I watched my brother lick the young marine's biceps where they protruded from the marine's short-sleeved shirt. He had to lick first one arm then the other as the marine stood to attention the whole time. Then the officer slowly undid the marine's fly and pulled out his big black 9" circumcised cock.

'OK, you limey shithead, on your fuckin' knees and get this all-American cock in your mouth. Suck all the U.S. Marine jizz out of it and we may spare your worthless life,' said the officer, as he turned and marched over to where I was standing.

'Look into this marine's eyes, boy, what do you see?' said the officer, as I gazed into the young cadet's blue eyes. 'I tell ya what, you see - hate, boy! Hatred of limey shit like you and all you stand for. He's risking his life for his country and ungrateful scum like you try to get in his way. He could bayonet you to death right now if I give the order.

Get up close and smell him, boy! What do you smell?'

'I smell U.S. Marine, sir!' I said truthfully, for the young kid as I got real close just smelt of clean uniform freshly laundered, soap and the clean masculine tang of America's fighting men. I too was made to lick the young marine's neck and biceps. This really turned me on, and by the time I was made to kneel in front of his long slim circumcised cock sticking like a ramrod straight out of his trouser fly I had a raging rock hard erection myself from the smell and taste of this All-American marine. I was full of lust for him and yearned to drink his delicious spunk.

'Suck that marine cock as if you're very life depending on it, 'cos it does! If you two don't bring these marine cadets off in two minutes flat I'm gonna order them to kill you. Now SUCK! Get those marine cocks right down your throats, and suck out their sweet teenage marine honey!'

Eight inches of young cadet marine cock was rammed down my throat, as hard as steel. It almost choked me, but I kept working it and sucking as hard as I could. Presently my marine started moaning, and I could hear my brother's marine moaning too. The cock in my mouth suddenly erupted with a volcanic flow of hot spunk which tasted more delicious than anything I'd ever tasted before. I swallowed it greedily, mouthful after mouthful of it. I then glanced at my brother and saw he was swallowing marine spunk too. Some of it overflowed on his chin.

'You, over here. Help your brother. Lick up that marine cum he's spilling, it's too good to waste!' ordered the officer. I had to kneel down and lick the marine spunk off my brother's chin.

'Your brother's not such a good cocksucker as you,' said the officer, 'That's cos you're a faggot, and he's a real man. But we'll break him yet. Till he learns to swallow the whole load from spurtin' marine cocks you'll have to lick up the overflow. If one bit of marine cum lands on the floor, you're both dead!' said the officer.

He then marched my brother and me thru a doorway marked RAPE ROOM #6 into a large hall with strange pieces of equipment in it and marines standing around in full uniform.

'See that sign on the wall, read it out loud!' said the officer, pointing to an official looking sign which covered the upper part of the far wall.

My brother and I read the sign out loud in unison: 'U.S.M.C. RAPE ROOM #6. Marines: Enjoy your rapes! Prisoners: Submit to the occupying forces! You are here to serve! You are just fuckmeat for the United States Marine Corps.'

'That's right, what are you?' asked the officer, blowing cigar smoke in our faces.

My brother and I replied in unison: 'We are just fuckmeat for the United States Marine Corps'.

'OK, boys, strap 'em to the double-spit roaster!' said the officer.

My brother and I were then strapped face down side by side to a kind of slanted padded leather table with our heads at the upper end. Two big

black marines then came up behind us and pulled our trousers down. They started slapping grease all over our backsides.

'Grease their limey asses up well, they're not used to taking big U.S. Marine cocks yet' said the officer.

'Y'all shoo has a cute little ass, honey,' said the black marine greasing me up, 'Would y'all like mah big black marine cock to open it up real wide, white boy? Ah'm from Texas, and everything's bigger in Texas, y'all better believe it, sweetie!'

If I didn't believe it, I soon did, as he rammed what must have been at least 12 solid inches of thick marine manmeat right up my 'ass' as he called it, and tearing it to pieces in the process.

'Shit, man - y'all done gotten blood all over mah cock!' said the marine, as he pulled his prick out then rammed it back in again, 'Why didn't y'all tell me I was poppin' yo' goddamn cherry, boy?'

My brother was also being raped by a big black cock, and he was screaming with pain. He really was a virgin as he had always done the fucking before, with girls.

'Shut up, mutha fucker,' said a tall white marine as he climbed some steps and shoved his big cock in my brother's mouth, 'Suck on this big teat, baby, it's gonna feed you sweet mother's milk that'll make you goo like a baby for more.'

The marine started fucking my brother's mouth, whilst another tall marine climbed up some steps and waved his big white cock in my face as I was still being fucked by the huge black prick up my 'ass'.

'Y'all hungry, boy?' he asked me. I nodded and opened my mouth to receive his cock. It tasted so good. Even though I had sucked 100 British army cocks on the parade ground that morning, these American cocks were something special. 'I done brought this all the way from Macon, Georgia just for you, boy!' he said as he fed me his meat. He fucked my mouth while the big marine fucked my 'ass', which by now was truly broken in and had learned to accept his huge meat. Then the guy fucking my face pulled out and said: 'Have y'all ever tasted a Georgia peach, boy?' and he made me take both his tight balls in my mouth at the same time. 'Oh yeah, suck those Georgia peaches -

they're done fulla sweet juice for you, boy. I'm gonna feed it to y'all real soon. Just keep on suckin' them peaches!'

I sucked and sucked on his nuts, then he rammed his cock in my mouth again, and sure enough he was soon feeding me the sweetest, creamiest man-milk I'd ever tasted. I swallowed it down greedily, aware that my brother was having trouble dealing with the cock in his mouth. It started spurting spunk and it was overflowing from my brother's mouth all over his chin and down his neck.

'Help yo' brother out,' said the marine who had just fed me, 'Lick up that big Yankee boy's cream that's spilling from his mouth and runnin' down his neck. Don't y'all waste none!'

I leaned over and licked the spunk from my brother's lips and chin, then moved down to his neck where a thick river of spunk flowed. God, it was so erotic licking my brother's smooth spunky neck as he kept swallowing the marine's cum. I almost came myself. Meanwhile the two marines fucking our 'asses' were near to climax.

'OK, honey, time to get pregnant. Would y'all like a boy or a girl?' said the black marine who had torn my 'ass' to pieces as he prepared to shoot. 'Here cums mah baby-juice, shootin' right up yo' lily white ass, boy!'

I felt his cum shoot right up me. Meanwhile another marine had shoved his cock in my mouth, and had started to cum almost immediately, so I was being fed marine spunk at both ends at the same time.

Finally my brother and I were unstrapped from the rape table, and the officer took us back to the outer room to await the British soldiers who were taking us back to our hut for the night.

'That was just a taster, boys" said the officer. 'Next time you'll be here for a whole day, and raped by marines from 9 till 5. We gotta break you in gradually - some of our boys are real big!'

The British soldiers arrived and we were taken back to our hut for the night. The first full day of my life at this army base hand ended, and all I had been fed was army spunk, piss and dog-food contaminated with cum. Was this all my life was to consist of from now on?

in rivers of lust, whilst the commanding officer shouted: 'That's right, fill him up with U.S. Marine cum, boys! Keep pumpin' him full of Marine jizz till he smells of cum like a horny sperm shooting U.S. Marine himself!' God it was so erotic, and the officer was right. These U.S. Marines DID smell spunky! The reeked of the hot cum they were shooting down our throats and up our arses. They also spunked in their underwear, as we were often made to lick them clean. They were always thick with dried cum, and often we were treated to some nice fresh juicy sperm as well in their jock-straps and briefs. These marines were so horny, they just stood and creamed their underpants all the time.

I was now used to this subservient military way of life. It was sheer depraved filth day after day. From being a pacifist who detested the military and all it stood for, I was still a pacifist, but one who now hero-worshiped the big butch real men in the British Army and the United States Marine Corps.

All we were ever given to eat and drink either came out of a soldier's cock, or had been contaminated by something which came out of their cocks. And I loved it. I was in Heaven amid all this filth!

One day some British army cadets were brought to the base for a day's training. They were all teenagers, looking very handsome in their cadet uniforms. In the afternoon I and my fellow captives were taken into a big hall on the base, filled with soldiers and U.S. Marines sitting in chairs. There were 20 of us male captives, and we were led by our chains on to the stage, at the back of which had been placed a huge banner reading: 'CADET TASTING COMPETITION'

The commanding officer then opened the proceedings.

'Now place your bets, men,' he said addressing the soldiers and marines in the audience. 'Which captive can drink the most cadet spunk? That's one bet. The other bet is which cadet will be voted as having the tastiest cum by the captives?'

The cadets were led on, all 60 of them, each carrying a card with a number on it. After all the bets were placed, we were made to kneel in front of the first rank of 20 cadets. They were then told to take their cocks out, and we had to suck them off.

The smell and taste of this cadet's cock was something else. His whole body seemed to reek of spunk! I couldn't wait to taste his load. It wasn't long before I was rewarded with 10 hot mouthfuls of delicious cadet cream, and it tasted every bit as good as he smelt!

'Like the taste of my orgasm, do you?' asked the cadet, 'Drink it all down. You'll be dreaming of my tasty load for the rest of your life. It's not for nothing I'm called Tasty-Load Taylor!'

I had to admit his spunk was the tastiest I had ever sampled, and indeed he went on to win the Tastiest Cadet competition, voted top by 18 out of the 20 of us prisoners.

We worked our way thru all 60 cadets, but although there were 20 of us we got more than 3 cadets each. These were young lads in their sexual prime, and each one was able to cum over and over again. During the next two hours I sucked off 23 different cadets, and swallowed all their loads. I didn't win the title of greediest cum drinker, though.

The Cum Drinkin' Champion this afternoon was my brother. They'd really broken him and turned him into a cum-drinking slut. He guzzled down 32 loads of cadet spunk in two hours and was till gagging for more when the competition finished. He had to be taken backstage and fed more cadet spunk off-stage to stop him screaming for more semen! It really was obscene to see his face covered in spunk and his cum-filled mouth screaming: 'Spunk, spunk... feed me more sweet cadet cum! More, more, I want more cadet sperm to drink!'

He then was given a special t-shirt to wear; the slogan on it read: 'Cadet Cum Drinking Champion - 60 loads.' He'd sucked off the other 28 cadets backstage. Lucky bugger, wish I could have managed it, but I just had to have a rest. After the 100 soldiers I'd already sucked off on the parade ground that morning, I just couldn't manage more than 23 cadets. Their spunk was so thick and sweet - and rich food didn't agree with my stomach!

Of course an hour later I was wishing I could have sucked off the other 37 cadets as well, but I'm sure they'll be back, or another cadet troop will visit the base next month for tasting.

Cadet Tasty-Load Taylor was given a special medal depicting a cum-spurting cock, complete with spunk in white enamel shooting into an

open mouth. The medal was inscribed: 'Tastiest Cadet - Cdt Tasty-Load Taylor'.

I slept well that night, with my rich cadet food inside me. Nothing like the tasty orgasms of 23 teenage boys to make you feel well-fed and go to sleep happy and contented. I was almost purring like the cat which got the cream. My brother, on the other side of the hut, must have been reliving his experience in his dreams, as he kept shouting out: 'Delicious cum, mate — more please! More cadet spunk! More, more — please feed me more cadet sperm!'

What had the Army done to us? We were cum junkies and sex slaves, truly Army Property. And we all loved it!

CHARLIE AND THE TIME MACHINE

I do like a man in uniform, so I advertised for one on the Internet. I got a reply from a military man, who said he'd seen active service. I emailed back and told him to make sure he arrived in full military uniform ready to give me orders.

I was very naïve, and didn't even think of requesting a photo or asking for personal details, but then I didn't much care. So long as he was a soldier dressed in his uniform, that was good enough for me.

I looked forward with increasing anticipation as the day and then time arrived for his visit. I had many wanks in the days beforehand thinking of what this big, butch soldier would order me to do, and the various ways he would make me pleasure him. I imagined every fetish and sexual position possible.

Finally the day arrived, and as the hour approached I got increasingly nervous, but also excited. He was 10 minutes late arriving, which I thought a bit odd for a soldier, but even stranger was the time he took from the entry door to my block of flats to my front door. Perhaps he got lost I thought, and was just about to go and look for him when my front doorbell rang. I glimpsed thru the spyhole, and saw a scarlet uniform.

'Oh, he's come in ceremonial guards' uniform,' I thought to myself. I'd have preferred khaki, but what the heck – it might be fun to have sex with a guardsman in his ceremonial uniform.

I opened the door and – shock, horror! In front of me stood a Chelsea Pensioner well into his 80s or possibly even in his 90s, in the scarlet and black uniform of the veterans who live at the Royal Hospital Chelsea. He had a walking-stick, and could hardly stand up, was out of breath and shaking with exhaustion.

'Ooh, them bleedin' stairs,' he wheezed (I was only up one flight) 'they nearly killed me. Must sit down.' And he pushed past me, and hobbled across the hallway into my lounge where he collapsed in an armchair.

I saw something orange on the floor in the hallway, and bent down to pick it up. It was his senior citizen's Freedom Pass giving him free travel on public transport, so I picked it up and gave it to him.

'Oh thank you, couldn't go anywhere without that,' he said, then gave me my first military order: 'Get an old soldier a nice cup of tea, two sugars please!'

What could I do? I went in the kitchen and made some tea, found some biscuits and sat down on the sofa with this old boy, sipping tea and chatting about his experiences back in the Second World War.

He was, in fact, 90 years old, so was 20 when World War II broke out. He showed me a photo of when he was first called up, aged 18. Even in the old-fashioned uniform with the 1930s Brylcreemed hairstyle, he looked really handsome, and I'd have certainly had sex with him then, but not now. How could I tell him?

'Oh, I know what you're thinking,' he said. 'they all expect a young serving soldier and get quite a shock when I arrive on their doorstep.'

'Well, I'm sorry, but I was rather surprised,' I said with considerable understatement.

'I promise you I will give you a good time that you'll remember all your life,' said the old soldier. 'Nobody has ever complained yet. In fact they keep coming back for more.'

I found this very hard to believe, but the old man then went on to make a truly fantastic claim.

'After I left the army, I became a scientist and an inventor,' he said. 'I missed all my old comrades who died in the War, and I became obsessed. I got involved in Spiritualism, and contacted a lot of them thru mediums. According to how the mediums described my old friends, they had apparently remained young, fit and good-looking, as I got older and more decrepit.

Anyway I decided I was going to try to realize H. G. Wells' fantasy and create a Time Machine to take me back to those days at the beginning of the Second World War, and finally I succeeded. Would you like to come back with me and see all the fun we had in the War? When we weren't actually fighting, it was going on everywhere. Here at home in the air raid shelters, parks, in the barracks and on the battlefields abroad. I'll show you if you like.'

Thinking the old man had completely lost his marbles, I politely thanked him, but said I thought I'd pass on his kind offer.

'You don't know what you'll be missing,' he said. 'I know you think I'm crazy, but why not just come along to my little laboratory and see for yourself. Can't do any harm can it?'

I thought about it, and what Heath-Robinson type contraption this nutty old professor might have built in some laboratory, and decided it might be good for a laugh, and it would humor the old chap, who was nice enough even if completely nuts. I was a muscular chap in my 40s, so even if he turned out to be a homicidal maniac I was confident I could overpower him very easily – indeed he could hardly stand up, and needed the aid of his walking-stick to remain upright.

So the following Saturday I traveled to the address he gave me, which was an allotment in Chelsea. He was waiting at the allotment gates,

in his scarlet Chelsea Pensioner uniform. I shook hands with him, we went in and I followed as he hobbled along the grass path between the plots, till we got to his one. There was a small tool-shed built up against the far wall of the allotments. He fumbled with some keys, and finally opened the door. As we stepped thru the door I was amazed – it was so big inside. It was like stepping into the Tardis, the Time Machine used by Dr Who in the TV series.

'Yes, we've already entered another dimensional space,' said the old chap. 'Time only exists as we know it in our own dimension. That machine over there is constantly ticking over, so the whole interior of the shed is in another dimension, outside of Time itself.'

This was incredible, but I had to admit the old boy was not crazy. Whether the odd looking contraption in the center of the room could really take us backwards and forward in Time or not, certainly something had happened already. The inside of the tool-shed was at least 20 times bigger than the outside, or we were 20 times smaller. Or else, as he claimed, we had entered another universe or dimension altogether.

He went over to the machine, flicked some switches and pressed some buttons, then told me to sit in a chair on the side of the equipment and strap myself in. He strapped himself in a similar one, but his had a control panel in front of it. Pulling some levers and setting some dials, the machine began to shake and emit a loud hum. Suddenly I felt giddy, and the tool-shed and everything else became a blur then disappeared altogether. I seemed to be in a spinning vortex, going down, down, down. It was quite scary, but in a few seconds it was all over, the machine stopped shaking and the hum died down to a slow whine. The tool-shed had disappeared, but the allotments were still there, bigger than before. We and the machine were in the middle of a grass patch, and all around us were vegetables of all kinds growing. I could see people in 1940s clothes gathering some of them – undoubtedly we were back in the Second World War, and this was part of the war effort in feeding the people from all available land.

I was amazed, and looked to my left to apologize to the old boy for doubting his sanity. He wasn't there. In his place in the controller's seat

was the young, handsome man I'd seen in the photo the old guy had showed me, just a few years older than when the photo was taken.

I unstrapped myself from my seat, so did he, and he came over and shook my hand.

'Well, congratulations! I'm astounded,' I said. 'You really did it, you've brought us back about 70 years to the Second World War.'

'1942 to be exact,' said the young soldier, who's name was Charles by the way. Though he preferred to be called 'Charlie'. 'As you see, I added a refinement so when visiting a time when I was alive, I can at the flick of a switch set the machine so I return to my age at that time. This makes sure people recognize me, and has other advantages. Now, when the next air-raid siren sounds, I'll show you what we soldiers did when home on leave.'

We left the allotment, and walked along the streets which looked much the same as in 2009. Only the gas lamp-posts and certain other things looked old-fashioned. Very few cars were on the roads, there was petrol rationing and few people could afford motor vehicles even in affluent Chelsea. We walked across Chelsea Bridge to Battersea Park, and I noticed the anti-aircraft guns and barrage balloons. We crossed Prince of Wales Drive with its posh mansions, and reached Battersea Park Road, which is fairly close to the railway lines leading into Clapham Junction Station, the busiest railway station in Britain. Here there was considerable bomb damage in the surrounding streets, worse as you got nearer the railway, which was obviously the target for Luftwaffe bombers.

'I lived in Battersea with my parents and sisters,' said Charlie. 'Never thought I'd end up across the River in the Royal Hospital.'

He was going to take me to meet his parents and sisters. I thought I would look very odd in my 21st Century clothes, but when I looked down at myself I saw I had miraculously been re-styled in the clothes of the period. I felt my balding head, and was amazed to find I had a full head of greasy, Brylcreemed hair combed back with a parting on the left.

'Oh don't worry, I also built that facility into my Time Machine,' said Charlie. 'No good arriving in 1942 looking like aliens from another planet. We'd be locked up as German spies straight away.'

As we walked down the street towards the area where his family home was, there was the wailing of the air-raid sirens.

'Now you'll see what I mean,' said Charlie, as he wheeled round and headed for Battersea Park again. Here there was a public air-raid shelter, and Charlie explained that with Chelsea Barracks so near across the River, and so many soldiers arming the anti-aircraft guns in the park, there'd be plenty of young military men down the shelter.

We descended with a lot of civilians and soldiers into the musky, damp darkness of the air-raid shelter. It was very dimly lit, and Charlie led me over to a particularly dark corner, where a lot of soldiers, sailors and airmen in full uniform were gathered.

'This area's reserved for military men, and their admirers,' said Charlie.

As my eyes got accustomed to the darkness, I was aware of people on their knees in front of these military men. I was shocked and amazed. Civilian men, and a few women, were giving blow-jobs to the soldiers, sailors and airmen in this dark corner of the huge air-raid shelter.

'I could do with a good gammeroosh', said Charlie, using an old fashioned word for a blow-job. I didn't need telling twice. I fell to my knees, unbuttoned the young Charlie's flies (this was long before zip fastener flies), and started sucking on his delicious young soldier's cock. As Charlie moaned in the darkness, I could hear the other military men moaning in ecstasy all around me. To my right was a guy sucking off a sailor. I heard the sailor moan, and dimly saw his spunk shoot out all over the guy's face and in his mouth. Then a soldier behind me moaned as he reached a climax, and his hot load shot all over my hair. This was absolute decadence, yet the other civilians in the shelter were either unaware of what was going on in this dark corner, or simply didn't care.

I continued sucking Charlie's cock, and suddenly he shuddered and whispered: 'I'm cummin', I'm cummin'...' as he shot a huge load of sweet soldier sperm into my mouth and down my throat.

I stood up, wiping the excess cum off my lips and chin, but Charlie said: 'You're not finished yet. There are loads of other soldiers, sailors and airmen waiting to be serviced, get on your knees and do your job – these boys are fighting and risking their lives for you. Show them some respect!'

He pushed me down to my knees again, and a Royal Air Force officer stepped up to me, unbuttoned his fly, took out his huge cock and barked: 'Suck on this, and make it good!' I sucked on the airman's big cock, and as I did so a sailor came over to my left and offered me his cock, and a soldier unbuttoned to my right and stuck his cock in my face too. I had to suck on all three cocks in turn – in fact all three tried to insert their penises into my mouth at the same time, stretching it impossibly.

'OK, I'm ready,' said the air force officer. 'Make sure you swallow all this air force semen, it's on ration so don't waste it!' With that he started spurting hot cum into my mouth. This is disgusting, I thought, but no sooner had he unloaded into my mouth, than the sailor stuck his cock into it and started unloading his creamy orgasm. 'How d'ya like the taste of a seaman's semen, matey?' he asked, and I could only say: 'Mmmmm!' as my mouth was full of the air force officer's and sailor's spunky loads.

Then the soldier barked: 'Open up, I want to feed you too,' and his big prick pumped a hot, thick load of soldier's spunk into my already overflowing mouth. I swallowed this huge cocktail of military cum from the three armed services, and got shakily to my feet feeling I had already done my duty for my country and its servicemen.

However, in the next 20 minutes or so I sucked many more military cocks to completion, and was fucked, without condoms of course as this was long before AIDS, by at least a dozen military guys in full uniform, I lost count exactly how many.

Staggering to my feet, full of cum at both ends, and almost unable to walk, Charlie led me over to the civilian section, and I was amazed in the better light here to see men and women having full sexual intercourse in public view. Nobody seemed to care or bat an eyelid.

Charlie explained: 'You're shocked, I can see. You won't read about this in the history books. But these people could all be dead tomorrow. A direct hit from a bomb would kill us all right now. They are grabbing every bit of pleasure when and where they can. And after all, what else can you do in an air-raid shelter, or in a blackout. You see why parents are reluctant to bring their kids down here, the ones who haven't been evacuated to the countryside. Kids use the private Anderson and Morrison shelters in people's gardens and kitchens, or else are taken down the Underground stations. These air-raid shelters were the darkrooms of the 1940s.'

As I stood there, opened mouthed with amazement, I felt my own fly buttons being undone. 'Oh no,' I thought. 'Not a woman!' I looked down, and saw a young man in civilian clothes, obviously on leave or exempt from the call-up, taking out my cock and then I moaned in ecstasy as the young blond started giving me an exquisite blow-job. His warm mouth expertly milked my now rock-hard cock, and Charlie whispered in my ear: 'Feed the young man. He's been kicked out of the army for being too outrageously gay. He sucked off every soldier in his barracks, and even dropped to his knees every time an officer approached him.'

I couldn't hold back, and shot my load into the young guy's willing mouth. He got up, and politely thanked me for feeding him. Then he turned round and went down on another guy.

'This is totally unbelievable,' I said to Charlie. 'I had no idea this is what you all got up to in the War.'

'Oh, you haven't seen anything yet,' said Charlie. 'Wait till the black-out tonight. It goes on everywhere then.'

He was right. We stuck around till after dark, and it was pitch black. People moved about with tiny torches (flashlights) with a pinpoint of light directed towards the ground. There were no street lights on, and

no light came from the windows of houses due to the black-out curtains. As we crept along the dark streets, we could see people having sex everywhere. Men and women up against walls and hedges, men with men (many in uniform), and women with women. Even when we got on a bus to go back across the River to Chelsea and the allotments, two men were at it on the back seat on the upper deck, one giving the other a blow job in the dimly lit interior with its blacked out windows, just a tiny hole to see where you were. The bus conductor came upstairs, took their fare and gave them a ticket without batting an eyelid – he just said: 'Enjoying yourselves, are you? You can suck me off when you've finished doing him!'

Sure enough, as we crossed Chelsea Bridge and got off the bus, the man who had been giving his friend a blow-job, was sucking on the bus conductor's cock.

Such depravity everywhere. Charlie explained once again: 'People seem to think that free love and moral decadence started in the Swingin' Sixties. It has always gone on, from very ancient times. Especially in wartime. In the Second World War, as you have seen, anything and everything happened. I could show you a lot more if we had time. Under Admiralty Arch at night you could get golden showers – piss all over you or in your mouth if you wanted. Whatever your fetish, whatever your sexual orientation, whatever your age you could get it in the Second World War and in the 20 years or so afterwards. Guardsmen were so poorly paid, they sold sex to men of any age in St James's Park, Hyde Park and all over the place. And they didn't charge much either, they were glad to get a blow-job from anyone. After the War women weren't so free and easy and willing to oblige, not till the Pill came long in the 60s anyway.'

We reached the allotment and Charlie's Time Machine. We strapped ourselves in, and all too soon were back in the boring (by comparison) 21st Century, where outside of gay backrooms and similar places, everyone seemed to behave in a very respectable, civilized manner. But you can bet I'll be visiting Charlie and his Time Machine again in the near future. I wonder what filthy era he'll take us back to next time? Or maybe forward to some future decadence? The mind boggles!

POLICE FRAME-UP

Introduction

This is a fictional story, a sado-masochistic fantasy. It does not reflect on the real nature of British police forces, and I've never heard any evidence that they have gone to the extreme lengths described in this story. However they used to be very homophobic.

My partner, when homeless in London and living as a rent boy, was sleeping rough near the Royal Festival Hall and was awoken by a policeman in uniform who ordered my partner to give him a blow-job or be arrested; presumably for prostitution and vagrancy. On another occasion he was arrested in a public toilet with another man, and when he protested they weren't doing anything the police said: 'No, we know you weren't, but if we hadn't come in when we did you might have done something.' They then framed them both with false evidence. On yet another occasion they arrested him in a public toilet along with his best friend, another rent boy, and accused them of picking each other up. It was ridiculous; they'd lived together for years as 'sisters' and never had what was then known as 'tootsie trade'. They had no need to go to a public convenience if they wanted to have sex together, as they often shared a bedroom.

I was once arrested for an offense in a public toilet - there were no gay clubs to go to then in UK which allowed sex on the premises and it was illegal to even proposition another man for sex - and in the police station, when I mentioned my rights, I was told I had none and was threatened with being beaten up by the police.

This story just takes these incidents to the extreme, and turns them into a sexual fantasy, part of which I have acted out with two young men dressed in a police uniforms on separate occasions. I have also given a uniformed policeman a blow-job in a toilet. Another two policemen who caught me loitering in a toilet with a glory-hole in it said I needed a good fucking, but sadly they never obliged. The British police are now much more tolerant of gays, and the law now allows gay sex clubs, pornography, etc..

End of introduction, so now read my fictional story.

The Story

It was in the late 1980s, long after the 1967 Sexual Offences Act which supposedly legalized male homosexuality in Britain (lesbianism had never been outlawed because Queen Victoria refused to believe it existed or that women would do such things!) The 1967 Act only made homosexuality legal if not more than two males over the age of 21, neither of them in the armed forces, found themselves alone in a locked bedroom with nobody else present anywhere else in the house, apartment, mansion, castle or palace. It could be a 200 room mansion, but if someone was present in one of the other 199 rooms, you could be arrested. This law made all gay clubs which allowed sex on the premises illegal.

It was also illegal to proposition another man, either by approaching him in a bar, a gay club or in any public place, or by putting an advertisement in the press. Like prostitution, the act itself, if under the circumstances described above, was not illegal, but any possible way of prostitute and client meeting or two men meeting and arranging to have sex, was illegal. The charge for smiling at or flirting with another man in a gay bar, etc. was 'importuning for an immoral purpose'.

So when I was arrested in a public toilet which I had just gone into for a genuine purpose, I knew I was in trouble. I had a police record for 'indecent behaviour' as homosexual acts were described in law at the time, having been arrested in cruising grounds and public toilets before. But this time I was completely innocent. There was one other person in the toilet, a lad of about 18, but he was right the other side from where I was standing. We were both arrested, and I, being 22, was accused of corrupting a minor.

'We'll throw the book at you this time,' said the arresting officer at the police station. 'That boy is under-age, so that makes you a rapist and a child molester'.

'Hang on a minute,' I protested. 'In the first place, we weren't doing anything. He was nowhere near me. In the second place, if he's 18 as you say he is, then that makes him just 4 years younger than me, and old enough to die for his country in a war. Hardly a child, surely?'

'Don't get cocky with us, son!' sneered the young policeman.

'I know my rights, and I demand to make a phone call to my lawyer,' I said defiantly. I was fed up and wasn't going to take any more crap from the boys in blue.

There was another young policeman in the room, and he feigned a punch right into my face, but pulled short just before he made contact.

'You have no fuckin' rights in here, understand?' he snarled. 'You're just a dirty fuckin' queer who fucks little boys, and we're gonna stitch you up for a long prison sentence.'

Now I was really scared. Of course it was completely untrue. I'd never been interested in 'little boys', and hadn't even been doing anything with this 18 year old, who was far from a little boy. In fact I'd seen him around, and knew him to be a rent boy. I'd never been with him, but had seen him going into cubicles with older men, and had seen money exchange hands. I could have told the police this, but didn't want to get the lad into more trouble, so I kept quiet.

'Now we're going to present to the court cast iron evidence that you sodomized this young lad. The police doctor discovered your sperm inside his rectum', said the first policeman.

'B... b... but that's impossible!' I stammered. 'I never went anywhere near him.'

'Don't give me that,' said the second policeman, 'You were right up his arse when we came in. Disgusting behavior, reminded me of animals. Made me want to throw up!'

'That's not true!' I said, now really angry again, and my anger overcame my fear.

'You know it's not true, so do we, but the court won't know that. By the time we've fitted you up, you'll be found guilty, we'll make sure of that!' sneered the first policeman. 'Get the idea?' He laughed.

'Now do as we fuckin' tell you, or we'll make mincemeat out of you,' said the second policeman, who had already threatened me with violence.

'I feel like being sucked off, how about you Jamie?'

He was looking at the first policeman, who replied: 'I feel like a good shag. He's got a cute little bum, let's rape him at both ends! We haven't had any fun with a queer boy since last night, and I'm randy as Hell!'

I couldn't believe what I was hearing. These policemen were arresting me for homosexual acts which I hadn't even committed, yet were now threatening to rape me, and saying not only would they enjoy it, but that they had done this before.

'What? What are you saying? I don't understand? You can't be serious!' I said.

'Oh but we are dead serious,' said the first policeman. 'Are you thick or something? Don't you know where you are? You're in one of this police station's male rape rooms. We regularly rape queers in here. It's boring being a policeman, and we need a bit of fun as much as any other red-blooded males. Only difference is we can't be arrested for fucking other men, because we ARE the law!'

'That's right!; said the other policeman. 'We've raped hundreds of young men in here, many of them under age, and we fuckin' enjoy it! Your little friend, the 18 year old; you should have gone for his arse. He has a great bum. I've fucked it many times in here, I had him screaming with agony the first time, just after he turned 18. He never took it up the arse before I raped him, he just wanked off old men for a tenner a time.'

'Wanna see what's happening to him now?' asked the first policeman. Without waiting for me to answer he flicked a switch, and a CCTV screen came to life. It showed another room in the police station, and the 18 year old lad was being gang-raped by 6 policemen all in full uniform.

5 were taking turns to fuck his arse, and one had his huge cock in the youth's mouth. As I watched I saw the policeman in his mouth pull out and shoot 6 huge wads of spunk all over the lad's face. The others were still taking turns in fucking him.

They left the CCTV screen on, and the second policeman, who had blue eyes and short blond hair, came and stood in front of me and I could see he had a big erection inside his blue serge uniform trousers.

'Feel my big truncheon', he sneered. 'Go on, feel it inside my trousers. It's getting hard for your pussy-boy mouth.'

The other policeman, who had short red hair (neither of them could have been more than 25) spoke lecherously into my ear and started rubbing my crotch. I couldn't help it, I was getting a rock hard erection.

'Yes, you're getting excited aren't you, at the thought of being raped by two big butch policemen!' he said. 'Now feel PC Spink's big cock.

Feel it getting hard for you. Soon you're going to be drinking PC Spink's spunk. How do you feel about that?'

'I don't believe it, this can't be happening,' I said. 'You're police officers, you uphold the law. This sort of thing can't be happening in Britain'.

'Oh but it is happening, it happens every day,' said the redheaded police officer, 'And because we ARE the law, nobody can touch us. You should've joined the police force, son, then you could've raped as many young men as you liked. That's why we joined up.'

I felt the blond policeman's big cock thru his police trousers, and had to admit I was getting turned on, especially as the redheaded officer now had my cock out and was wanking it. He slowly rubbed his spit into the head, and cooed obscenely in my ear: 'Unzip PC Spink's big truncheon. He wants to feed you his hot policeman's cum.'

I unzipped the policeman's flies, and his long, smooth, circumcised prick sprung out, splashing delicious pre-cum all over my lips and face.

I couldn't help it, I licked my lips. I had never tasted a young policeman's cock juice before, and it tasted sweet. I wanted more!

'Yes, he likes the taste of your pre-cum, Bob,' said the redheaded policeman, 'I'd better stop wanking him or he'll shoot all over your uniform. I want to fuck his arse before he cums'.

Bob Spink pushed his cock head covered in pre-cum up against my lips, and my tongue involuntarily came out and obscenely licked the delicious slimy head. Slowly PC Spink's cock entered my mouth, and at the same time I felt the other policeman undoing the belt of my jeans.

'Stand up and lean over the desk', ordered the redheaded policeman who had now undone my jeans. Bob Spink pulled out of my mouth and I was made to bend across the desk, with my jeans around my ankles.

'Grease him up, Jamie,' said PC Spink, 'We'll spit-roast him. Ever been raped at both ends by two officers of the law, son? Aren't you excited? You're gonna be raped by two young policemen! PC Creamer is going to cream in your arse, while I cream in your mouth. You'll be pumped full of police spunk, son!'

I felt Jamie Creamer greasing up my arse, then felt his big cock slide in. At the same time Bob Spink rammed his big cock into my mouth again. The two policemen kept their uniforms on as they raped my arse and mouth, only their flies were open. My head was spinning with pure lust. This was a fantasy come true!

'You're sucking an officer of the law,' said PC Jamie Creamer. 'Do it well, and when he cums swallow all the police spunk he feeds you. Don't you dare spill any on his nice, clean police uniform. We don't want to shock any old ladies when we help them across the road with their shopping do we? They think our police are good decent men upholding the law, they don't know police stations are a den of perverted sex and depravity!' The policeman fucking my bum laughed as he said this, and PC Spink joined in.

'I can't hold out much longer,' said PC Spink, 'I'm about to blow my hot load of spunk right down his throat! Here it cums, son! Swallow this big load of thick police spunk!'

With that, his throbbing prick grew rigid and started pumping spurt after spurt of hot, thick spunk into my mouth and down my throat. All the time I could see the blue serge of his uniform in front of me; this was a policeman doing this to me, whilst another was still fucking my bum.

57

As though they read my thoughts, the two policemen reveled in the depravity of what they were doing: 'Yes, it's really happening. You're in a police station and an officer of the law is spunking in your mouth,' said PC Creamer as he continued fucking me. 'He's feeding you police sperm, drink it all down. You're drinking a policeman's orgasm in a police station rape room, disgusting isn't it? Didn't your mother tell you to always do what a policeman told you? Well fuckin' do it!'

'He loves the flavor of my orgasm, don't you, queer boy? He can't get enough of it. Swallow it all down, son, all that thick, sweet police semen. It's good for you. Aaaghh! Feels so goooood! Feedin' a queer my cum, and he's drinking it greedily like a baby guzzling its mother's milk!' said PC Spink as he shot another load of thick sweet police spunk right down my throat. I got a filthy thrill thinking I was doing what my mother told me, obey the police, but if only she could see what they were making me do!

'I'm about to pump his arse full of spunk,' said PC Creamer. 'Here it comes, boy! How d'ya like a policeman raping your arse and filling you full of his cum?'

I felt his hot load shooting into my arse, then he pulled out and they sat me down in the chair again.

'You look exhausted after being raped by just two policemen,' said PC Spink. 'Look at your friend on the screen. He's been raped by 6 policemen, so think yourself lucky this time! We'll have to break you in gently, but you'll be raped by all 20 policemen at this station before we're finished, then we'll pass you on to another police station to use.'

I couldn't believe this filth and depravity I was hearing from this young, good-looking, apparently decent policeman who I remembered had just last week helped my grandmother cross the road, and she had remarked what a nice policeman he was. If only she knew he had just orally raped her grandson, but worse was to come.

'He must be thirsty, Bob. Would you like a nice hot drink, son?' asked PC Creamer.

Now they'd had their wicked way with me, perhaps they were going to be nice to me, I thought. Thinking they were offering me a cup of tea, I said: 'Yes please, thank you.'

I thought I'd better be polite, but they weren't satisfied: 'Thank you, sir!' said PC Creamer. 'You're talking to officers of the law, show some respect to those who maintain law and order and a sense of decency. We protect society from depraved individuals like you. Now ask PC Spink nicely for a drink.'

'Please may I have a drink, sir!' I said, looking up into the blond policeman's big blue eyes. I saw no pity there; not an ounce of decency or humanity. Just a look of sheer depravity. He didn't even look at me as another human being; what he was seeing I was soon to find out.

'Of course you can, son. I've got a nice hot drink for you right here, open your mouth' he said, as he unzipped his fly again and stood in front of my chair.

'Open your mouth,' PC Creamer said in my ear, as he started jacking me off again. 'This nice policeman's going to give you a hot drink of his piss.'

'What! That's disgusting! You're policemen, you wouldn't do such a thing!' I said, genuinely shocked. They had to be joking, but no, PC Creamer stopped wanking me for a moment and slapped me across the face.

'Open your fucking mouth and be grateful for the hot drink PC Spink's going to give you,' he said, and recommenced jerking me off, using plenty of his spittle to make me moan. I opened my mouth in a groan of ecstasy as PC Creamer brought me to the verge of climax, and at that moment PC Spink started pissing straight into my mouth.

'Close your lips around my cock while I'm quenching your thirst!' said PC Spink, 'I don't want any fucking piss on my uniform! Keep swallowing my urine, that's right. That's quenching your thirst, isn't it? How d'you like the flavor of police piss, son? Your mouth and throat are just a police urinal. Look into my eyes, son, as I relieve myself in your mouth. That's right, drain all that piss like a good urinal. Ah, it feels so good, filling his mouth and belly with the contents of my bladder. Such a relief!'

That was it, the look he had given me before he started pissing down my throat. He saw me not as a human being, but as a urinal, his own personal toilet!

'Disgusting, isn't it?' said PC Creamer in my ear, as he watched me gulping down PC Spink's piss, and he continued to wank me off. 'He loves the taste of your piss, Bob. Look, he's gulping it down. He's really thirsty for a policeman's stinking urine! And he's cummin'; I'm making him cum. Quick get the sample beaker, Bob!'

I didn't know what he was talking about; sample beaker? But he was right about my loving the taste of the blond policeman's piss; it was strong and pungent, and overwhelming. I couldn't get enough of it, and it was so obscene and depraved, looking up into this handsome, blond policeman's blue eyes as he looked into mine and used my mouth as his personal toilet. That's all I was to him at that moment, yet he really was a law officer. I saw the word: `POLICE' in white lettering on his navy blue jersey as I looked up into his face; this was the force my parents had taught me to trust and respect, as standing for law and order and upholding standards of common decency. I saw PC Spink take a small plastic beaker from the table and hand it to PC Creamer.

Next thing I knew I was cumming. With PC Spink still pissing in my mouth, PC Creamer brought me to climax, and I shot a big load right into the plastic beaker he was holding over the tip of my cock.

'Right, we've got our sample!' said PC Creamer triumphantly. 'Know what this is, boy?'

'Yes, it's my cum,' I said, bewildered why they should want this in a beaker. Was it for some kind of medical test, I wondered.

'No, this is EVIDENCE! Evidence of the crime you committed in that toilet back there. Our police doctor found this semen, YOUR semen in the back passage of that under-age young lad out there. We've got you fair and square now.'

'What's more, son, he's found evidence that you've been drinking men's piss and spunk in that toilet. Your mouth and belly are full of it. Open up, I'm going to take some swabs' said PC Spink, who had finally finished pissing in my mouth.

They punched me and forced me to open my mouth, then took swabs. They said this was the evidence they needed to prove I'd not only fucked the 18 year old, but had also been doing disgusting things in the toilet with other men.

I felt trapped, and couldn't believe this was happening. Then PC Creamer spoke again: 'If you come up in court with this kind of evidence, particularly your sperm in the teenager's arse, you'll go down for a long stretch. But maybe you'd like that, being a fuckbag for some old lag in prison?'

'No, no. Please don't send me to prison!' I pleaded.

'Not up to us, it's up to the court,' said PC Spink, 'But the evidence we've got looks BAD, boy. Can you think of a way out of this mess for him, Jamie?'

'No, it looks very bad,' said PC Creamer. 'Unless; yes there might be a way out. If you report back here to this police station every evening at 6pm, then we won't prosecute.'

'You won't prosecute? Oh thank you,' I said, relieved.

'But you'll have to service all the policemen in this station every evening, until we tire of you. Then we'll pass you on to another police station for our colleagues there to use. You'll be drinking policemen's spunk and piss for at least 6 months, son. And be regularly gang raped up the arse by up to 20 officers. They'll be lining up for a cute bum like yours.'

Secretly, I was excited. I couldn't imagine a more exciting scenario. OK, some of the policemen may not be my type, but what the heck. I was going to have non-stop dirty sex from maybe a 100 or more uniformed policemen inside a police station for the next few months, maybe longer. What could be legally safer, or more exciting, than that? So long as I played ball (and played with THEIR balls) and gave them what they wanted, I wouldn't be arrested.

And I have always had a secret fantasy of being sexually abused by a uniformed policeman; now I was going to be raped and used as a urinal by a non-stop army of uniformed policemen, and all inside a police station. The thought of innocent passers-by thinking this was a place where standards of decency and morality were upheld by officers of the law, when all the time they were committing acts of the utmost depravity on innocent young men filled me with a warped sense of excitement. I was so happy I'd been 'arrested' that evening, and to be serving this police force in the most depraved manner anyone could imagine.

61

Following that first episode I enjoyed over 6 months of non-stop sado-masochistic sex with the police force. Since then I have never looked at policemen in the same way again. Maybe that was just one, corrupt police force, but I can't help wondering how many other apparently decent policemen are doing the same thing. I find myself smiling at young handsome policemen nowadays, and on more than one occasion it has paid off. Only last week I smiled at a young policeman in the park, and he pushed me into the park toilets, into a cubicle and forced me to suck him off. Last month in the same park a policeman raped me in the bushes.

As the old gay slogan shouted on gay marches went: '2-4-6-8, is that copper really straight?' From my experience, a lot of them aren't.

Thank goodness!

MAKE LOVE NOT WAR

This is a fictional, erotic and romantic set of short wartime stories with a strong political message, for which I make no apologies.

Episode 1 — On the Battlefield

It was during the Second World War, and like millions of others all over the world I'd been conscripted to fight for the old men who had started the whole thing. Old men like Churchill, Roosevelt, Stalin, Hitler, Mussolini and Emperor Hirohito, relatively safe in their underground bunkers, etc. whilst we youngsters, barely out of school, were sent out to kill each other.

I found myself on a battlefield in Southern Germany near the Swiss border. I'd been in several battles, and like some of my fellow soldiers I'd always deliberately fired my gun to miss the enemy, because I was basically a pacifist. I didn't care if I died, but I didn't want to be responsible for killing someone else's young son. I'd tried to avoid being called up, but they didn't believe me when I said I was a conscientious objector because I was an atheist with no religious beliefs.

Although I was a pacifist, I couldn't help thinking of the advice someone had given to young men made to fight old men's wars. I think it was Lenin who said they should turn their guns on their own officers. If all the young men on all sides fighting this war did that, or simply refused to fight or deserted to a neutral country, the war would be over tomorrow.

We had been ordered to 'mop up' after our battalion had attacked a village occupied by the Germans. Our orders were to take no prisoners, every German soldier we found was to be killed. I wasn't told the reason for this order, which was illegal, but knew it was not uncommon in wartime where all sorts of atrocities occur because the normal rules of decent human behavior have broken down. I'd seen men and children killed and the women raped, and my fellow soldiers laughed at me because I refused to take part in any of it.

'Look, here's a gorgeous young fraulein,' said my buddy after we entered one house and he had shot dead the woman's father and mother. 'Rape her, go on - she's begging for it.' I was horrified, but he had been brutalized by the army and the hatred, anarchy and inhumanity of war. As far as I was concerned, he was no better than the Nazis. Just a steely-eyed killing machine, as a British officer had proudly described every one of his men.

I thought of turning and walking away, but that wouldn't save the girl, who I feared would be killed after my buddy had finished with her. So I took her in the bedroom. My buddy wanted to come in and watch, and then rape her himself, but I locked the door behind me. The poor girl looked very scared, and was heartbroken because her parents had just been shot.

'Quick, climb out of the window!' I said. She didn't understand English, so I went over to the window and opened it. There were no soldiers around, and there was a forest a few yards away. She might stand a chance if she could make it to the trees. I pointed to the open window and said some of the few German words I knew: 'Ausgehen, schnell, schnell!'

She rushed to the window and made her escape. I watched her flee towards the trees, then I turned to the door, but heard something move beneath the bed. I stooped down and saw a young lad, about 18. He looked very frightened, and he had tears in his big blue eyes. I pulled him out from under the bed. 'Rape him!' The words came into my head,

for I was gay, and whilst I had no desire to have sex with women, this beautiful young lad with flaxen blond hair was giving me a rock-hard erection inside my uniform trousers. He was entirely within my power, and whatever I did to him there would be no come-back. As the victor in war, I could do what I liked with him. He looked down and saw my trousers sticking out obscenely, and looked even more scared.

'Bitte, nein, nein!' he pleaded.

Of course I wouldn't do it. Not unless he gave me some encouragement and wanted me to. I pointed to the window, and said the same thing to him: 'Ausgehen, schnell!' He made for the window, but before he climbed out he turned and kissed me full on the lips.

'Danke schen!' he said, then he climbed out and was gone. I watched him follow his sister safely into the forest.

I had some explaining to do when I unlocked the door and faced my buddy. I just said the window was open and the girl escaped. His reaction was that I should have shot her so there were no witnesses to the atrocity he had committed, but I told him my gun had jammed.

Now here I was in a similar situation, ordered to go into a German village and kill any enemy soldiers we found. Once in the village we came under sniper fire. In the confusion I was able to slip away from my fellow soldiers, and enter a house on my own. Inside, cowering behind the window, was a young German soldier, no older than me - about 18. Like so many German youths he was the Aryan ideal - blond hair, blue eyes - just my type. They really shouldn't conscript gays into the army, let alone pacifist gays. Did they really expect me to kill a beautiful guy like this? I'd rather he shot me instead.

When he saw me enter with my gun, he dropped his, put his hands up, cowered down and pleaded with me: 'Bitte, please - do not shoot!'

Obviously he thought other Allied soldiers were behind me and he was outnumbered.

My orders rang thru my head: 'Take no prisoners. Kill the Kraut bastards! Kill every one of them!'

I went over to the German soldier - he was trembling with fear. I put my gun down and reached out to him, but he pulled away, thinking I was going to kill him with my bare hands. He evidently knew some English, so I spoke to him: 'It's OK, I'm not going to hurt you. What's your name?'

'M... meine Namen? My name it is Karl, p... please don't kill me' he stammered.

I reached out and took hold of his hands. They were clammy with sweat. I pulled him up and towards me.

'It's all right, I'm not going to hurt you, I'm Jack. I'm your friend.' I said. What was I saying? How could I be his friend? I had been ordered to kill him, and the village was swarming with Allied soldiers. But I knew I had to try to save him.

Still he didn't quite trust me, his lips were trembling with fear. So I pulled him close to me, embraced him and kissed him on the lips saying: 'It's all right, I won't hurt you. We must escape.'

His reaction was instantaneous. The German soldier hugged me tight, and kissed me back. As we hugged, I could feel his cock getting hard thru his uniform, and he must have felt mine in the same condition. There, in the middle of the war-zone, this German soldier and myself started to make love. We kissed, we cuddled, we grinded our hips together. Then we undid out fly-buttons and jerked each other. I went down on him, and pretty soon a big German soldier's cock was shooting its cream into my mouth. I stood up, with my mouth full of this young lad's cum, and he returned the favor. He went down on me, and soon I was feeding him my load. We stood up again, and stared at each other, our lips covered with each other's sperm. We kissed again, exchanging the spunk in our mouths.

Suddenly there was a noise outside. I motioned him to be quiet, then I ran out to the front door. A British soldier stood there pointing a gun at me.

'It's OK, I've checked this building - nobody here!' I said, and the soldier turned and went. I then noticed a British army jeep outside, with a dead British soldier at the wheel. I motioned to Karl to stay where he was, and after I made sure the coast was clear, I ran to the jeep, pushed the

driver's body to one side, and started the engine. I drove the jeep over to the door of the house where Karl was hiding. I then man-handled the body of the dead British soldier out of the jeep and into the house.

With Karl's help we managed to strip him of his uniform. Then Karl got out of his uniform - God, he had a beautiful body! But I had little time for such carnal thoughts, and told him to put on the dead British soldier's uniform quickly.

He put on the clothes, but then turned to his discarded uniform and retrieved something from the pocket.

'Quick! We must go, hurry up. Schnell, schnell!' I said to him.

Now dressed as a British soldier, he climbed in the jeep beside me, and I started the motor. I drove out of the village, and headed for the Swiss border a few miles away. We saw few soldiers, either Allied or Axis troops, on the way. I just put my foot down and ignored everything and everyone, till we spotted the border post. We drove thru at full speed, some border guards shooting at our jeep as we passed. Once safely across and several miles into Switzerland, we abandoned the jeep, and walked to the nearest village. We were going to make for the police station and claim asylum in this neutral country.

As we were walking thru the woods on our way from the jeep into the village, we stopped for another love-making session. It was beautiful. We achieved full penetration this time - I fucked Karl, and then he fucked me. After we had both climaxed inside each other, we just lay there cuddling and kissing for about an hour.

'Ich liebe dich, I love you' said Karl, and I told him how much I loved him too.

'What was it you took out of your uniform pocket back in the house?' I asked him.

Karl smiled, and took out of his pocket a little wallet. Inside were some photos. His mother, father, sister, brother and their little pet dog. I then showed him the photos of my own family which I carried in my pocket.

I thought how crazy this war was - here we were, two young lads who were ordered to kill each other, yet we were so similar. We had

no reason to hate each other, we had just been conscripted into our respective countries' armies, we had no say in the matter. It was old men who led us into this war, and old men who gave the orders to the troops in their command to kill, rape and destroy.

When I saw the photos of Karl's family it brought home to me that all the German soldiers fighting this war were some mother's son. Many of them were not real Nazis, they were just conscripts. We didn't then know the full horror of the Nazi concentration camps, but I did know the Nazis were brutal thugs. But my Karl was no Nazi, I knew that.

'Don't worry, you'll see your family soon, when the war is over,' I said.

Then Karl said something which broke my heart: 'No, I'll never see them again. They are all dead. They died in a British air-raid,' he said, as tears rolled down his cheeks. I held him close to me and kissed away his tears.

'Oh, I'm so sorry!' I said, 'The murdering bastards! The RAF - bloody war criminals. Why do they have to bomb innocent civilians?'

After the war we learnt of the firestorm, started by British incendiary bombs, which destroyed the beautiful city of Dresden, and similar controversial air-raids on Hamburg and Berlin which killed thousands of civilians - men, women and children. The British airmen who carried out these raids, and the Americans who dropped atomic bombs on Hiroshima and Nagasaki, never faced a tribunal and were never punished for their heinous war crimes. Instead they are still feted as heroes. Bomber Harris, who along with Churchill ordered the British air-raids, even has a statue erected to him in London.

It still makes me feel sick that nobody on the Allied side was tried for killing indiscriminately thousands upon thousands of innocent civilians. These war crimes went unpunished, and this is what is known as 'Victors' Justice'.

Karl then apologized to me for what the Luftwaffe, unmanned flying bombs and V2 rockets had done to cities like London and Coventry, committing war crimes against the British people. We hugged again, and then made our way to the village and asylum from this crazy war. Whatever happened, whoever won the war, we were all human beings with families of our own. If only we could remember that, and reach out

to each other, ignoring the old men who told us to fight for our country, or for this cause or that cause. If only we could remember our humanity and forget the rest, as the philosopher Bertrand Russell said.

If only, like Karl and myself, we could learn to make love, not war!

It is now 60 years since the war ended. Karl and I are still lovers. We are in our late 70s, and living in an old people's home in Munich. We still share a bed. I am so glad I never followed orders over 60 years ago - Karl was the best thing that ever happened to me, and he says the same thing about me.

Episode 2 — Under Occupation

(The description later in this story of life in the German Democratic Republic – East Germany – is a fairly accurate one. Homosexuality was legalized in 1968 and much more liberated than in London, England at that time. The GDR was also a multi-party state, although they were all in a coalition government led by the Marxist-Leninist SED or Socialist Unity Party.)

The scene is St Helier, capital of Jersey in the Channel Islands, during the Second World War. Our group of islands, in the Channel off the coast of Northern France, were the only part of the British Isles to be occupied by German troops. I was 18 when the Occupation took place, living with my parents in a big house on the edge of town.

When the Germans came, several of their soldiers were billeted to stay in our house. We were lucky, some of those with even bigger houses had them requisitioned for the German occupying troops and the former residents had to live elsewhere. We were allowed to stay, and my mother (there was no women's liberation in those days) was expected to cook, clean and wash laundry for both her family and the German soldiers staying with us.

I must admit I was quite excited at the thought of German soldiers, in fact ANY soldiers, staying in our house. I was at the height of my teenage sexual development, and I knew I was definitely much more interested in men than in girls. What's more, the sight of a uniform, especially a smart one like the Germans wore, made me just want to roll over and surrender without a struggle!

Four young German soldiers were to stay with us, three in the spare bedroom, and Praise Be, one to share my bedroom! When they arrived, my heart skipped a beat. They were all extremely handsome in their uniforms, but I immediately picked the one I wanted to share my room. He was three years older than me, tall, blond, and he winked at me the

day they arrived, as their commanding officer gave instructions to my parents.

I quickly found out his name - Wolfgang. I lost no time in telling my mother I wanted him to be the one to share my bedroom.

'It's up to them,' said my mother, 'We are in no position to give orders.'

Never one to be slow, I took the first opportunity to invite Wolfgang to share my bedroom, and he agreed.

'Ja, zat vould be zehr gut,' he said in his broken half-English.

I put my hand out to shake his, and said: 'Friends?'

'Ja, friends!' he smiled at me as he shook my hand.

Already I was treading on dangerous ground. Fraternizing with the enemy. We were supposed to be cool and keep our distance, just doing what was absolutely necessary, not making the Germans feel welcome. I didn't care - I went out and bought four bunches of flowers and gave some to each of our German guests. That's how I looked on them, as foreign guests who had come to stay, and who deserved our hospitality. True they were uninvited guests, but I was determined to make friends with all of them, and hopefully become more than friends. The soldiers were delighted, if a little embarrassed, when I gave them the bunches of flowers. 'Von deine Mutter?' asked one. 'No, not from my mother - from me!' I said, pointing at myself. 'Von mich - Welkommen nach Jersey, Welkommen nach unsere haus - Welcome to our house!' They thanked me, and Wolfgang winked at me again and gave me a big smile. I felt I was well in there already.

There was a name in the Channel Islands for women who thought and acted the way I did. Young girls who threw themselves at German soldiers, and slept with them, were called 'Jerry-bags'. I was quite happy to be called a Jerry-bag or anything else the locals came up with. Four strapping soldiers staying in our house, all starved of sex and dying for a good fuck, and the most good-looking one actually sleeping in my bedroom. Of course I hoped I could entice him into sharing my bed, and the other three as well. I wasn't a whore - they charge for their services; I was willing to give mine for free. Nowadays I'd be called a 'slapper'. Back then most people were far too innocent to even dream

an 18 year old boy would get up to any hanky-panky with four male German soldiers.

My parents were worried about my sister, who was 15, so sent her to stay with our grandparents. They thought it was too much like tempting fate to have an adolescent girl around four soldiers, all sleeping under one roof. It never entered their heads that their son was only too glad his sister was out of the way, leaving the field open to him.

I freely admit my motives for 'fraternizing with the enemy' were mainly sexual; no way was I going to act coldly to these four gorgeous hunks of men staying in our house. I wanted sex with all of them, especially with Wolfgang. But there were other motives as well. They were just conscripts, like I would be in two years' time. I had no real quarrel with them. I was basically anti-war since it always seemed to cause more problems than it solved, and caused even more suffering.

After the Second World War ended I couldn't help reflect that it didn't save 6 million Jews and others from dying in the concentration camps. On the contrary the war, and especially the opening up of the Eastern front against the Soviet Union, probably sealed the fate of those in the camps. Hitler's Final Solution was not introduced until the War had been on some time, in fact after the Soviet Union had entered the war in 1941. Nobody was executed in gas chambers in the 6 years Hitler was in power before the War, nor for some time after it started. In war people can get away with anything.

It is just so much easier to hide and excuse atrocities such as genocide when there is a war on. German soldiers and citizens were dying every day; the whole German population was under constant bombardment. People were worried about their sons in the armed services and about themselves and their families being bombed; few people had much time to worry about what was happening to minority groups like the Jews, Gipsies, homosexuals, Communists and others who were shipped off to the concentration camps.

I also realized, after the War ended, how little it had solved. Britain went to War with Germany after first Czechoslovakia and then Poland had been invaded and occupied by the Germans. Austria had also been annexed. At the end of the War Czechoslovakia and Poland were still occupied, only this time by the Russians instead of the Germans. The victors of World War II carved Europe up between them at the

conferences at Yalta and Potsdam. The Soviet Union occupied the whole of Eastern Europe, and although most of these countries were nominally independent, they were kept in check by the Warsaw Pact alliance and Soviet troops for the next 44 years. Poland and Czechoslovakia only became genuinely free in 1989. Austria fared a little better - half of it, including its capital Vienna, was in the Soviet Zone until 1955, when the Russians marched out on condition Austria remained neutral. If Britain went to war to save Poland, then it was a total failure. All we achieved for the Poles was to exchange the dictator-occupier Hitler for Stalin!

None of this was any surprise to me. Wars rarely achieve their objective, and never achieve real peace or democracy. The First World War sowed the seeds of the Second. The unfair Treaty of Versailles imposed on the Kaiser's defeated Germany led directly to the eventual rise of Hitler and the Nazis. The Second World War resulted in the division of Europe into two blocs, and the dangerous Cold War which could have gone nuclear and destroyed the world. Thankfully it didn't, though we had some near scrapes, including the Berlin crisis of 1961 and the Cuba crisis of 1962.

Back to occupied Jersey, I had mixed emotions. I didn't like the idea of my country being occupied, and I was concerned about the fate of my Jewish friends. I decided I would do my best to help them, but I wasn't about to join any Resistance movement which I thought would only give the Germans an excuse to commit more atrocities. My approach was complex. To befriend the ordinary German conscript soldiers, and try and get `my oats' from them at the same time, whilst being prepared to act to save my Jewish friends if I possibly could, and to try to stop any atrocities being committed by anyone. I had a gun, which I hid inside my mattress, but hoped I'd never have to use it. My pacifism didn't extend to standing by, however, and watching my family and friends being killed or taken away to death camps. I was willing to die trying to stop any atrocities occurring, but I wasn't willing to kill ordinary German conscripts so long as they weren't actually threatening anybody.

It was not an easy path to steer, but I determined I'd try to do my best. My main strategy was to win the hearts and minds of the German occupiers; to look on them as guests in my country rather as 'the enemy' and hope this would make them less trigger happy. Occupation armies under constant threat of attack from 'terrorists' or 'resistance/freedom fighters' commit more atrocities, because of fear and the desire for revenge. That was my reasoning anyway. I would only use violence as a very last resort to save innocent lives.

Meanwhile, I had other things on my mind. First of these, was how to get Wolfgang into my bed. The first night the soldiers stayed with us, Wolfgang came into the bedroom and sat on his bed. He offered me a cigarette, but I didn't smoke.

We talked for a while. I asked about his family, and he showed me photos of his parents, brothers and sister. He came from Rostock, in the northeast of Germany.

After about half an hour he got undressed, carefully hanging up his smart uniform so it wouldn't crease. I climbed into my bed and watched as he slowly revealed his muscular body. It was like having my own private striptease show here in my own bedroom. I couldn't help myself, I was playing with my cock beneath the bedclothes. Wolfgang was sure to notice, but I didn't care. I had a rock-hard erection, and I knew he must have seen it before I got into bed. My underpants were sticking out as though a tent-pole were inside them!

'Ist kalt - it's cold,' said Wolfgang as he climbed into his bed.

There was my opening, and I grabbed it boldly: 'You can share my bed,' I said like the brazen hussie I was, 'I'll warm you up.'

'Ja? You are a very naughty boy!' said Wolfgang, 'Do you say these things to lots of men?'

'I don't get the chance, living here with my parents,' I said truthfully, 'But yes, I've picked up men in the cottages... er, I mean in public toilets. Gone back with some of them.'

'A very naughty boy,' said Wolfgang. I wondered if I'd gone too far.

After all, known gay men were sent to concentration camps. But I had to have this gorgeous German soldier if I possibly could, even if it was the last thing I did. I was sure the whole Aryan ideal thing was homoerotic anyway, and I wouldn't even be surprised if Hitler was both bisexual and partly Jewish. I had met several boys at school who would beat up a queer one minute, and get him behind the bike sheds for some illicit gay sex the next. People are a mass of contradictions. Anyway, I was willing to risk my life to bed this handsome German soldier.

As I lay there wondering what would happen next, Wolfgang lit another cigarette. He was thinking, that was obvious. Presently he put out his smoke, got up and went over to the door. My heart missed beat - was he going to report me to his fellow soldiers, would I be taken away to a concentration camp as a sexual deviant? Or would he tell my parents, which was not that much better. I didn't know how they'd react. I could be in deep trouble with them and the police, now under German command.

However I heard the lock click as Wolfgang turned the key from the inside, so we wouldn't be disturbed. He then came over to my bed and said: 'I am cold - I share your bed tonight.'

'Every night,' I said, as I threw open the bedclothes to reveal my cock sticking out of my underpants like a ram-rod.

'You are big boy,' said Wolfgang, and I saw he had a growing erection too, much bigger than mine.

'So are you,' I said, looking directly at his cock.

'Naughty boys like you should be punished!' whispered Wolfgang, so that the soldiers and my parents in the adjoining bedrooms couldn't hear. 'How vould you like a big German soldier's cock to fuck you? You need a good fucking, turn over!'

I was in Heaven! Being ordered about by this big, muscular example of German manhood, this strapping blond soldier. I turned on to my stomach, and soon felt Wolfgang's big cock slowly entering my tight arse hole. The fact that this was happening with my parents in the next room, having sent their daughter away to preserve her virginity, gave me a depraved thrill. If only they knew their son was being fucked in the next bedroom by a German soldier!

'Aufmachen!' whispered Wolfgang in my ear, as he pushed his big prick into the entrance of my back passage. 'Open up, I am going to fuck ze shit out of you!'

I relaxed my anal muscles to let him enter, and Wolfgang lived up to his promise. He fucked me so hard, the bed was rocking like crazy. I wondered if my parents could hear in the next room, but I didn't really care. If I was a 'Jerry-bag' I liked it, and I hoped I would soon be filled

with hot German spunk. Wolfgang's stiff cock rammed even harder into my arse as he bit my ear and then whispered: 'Ich kumme jetz - I am cummin....'

I felt jets of hot spunk shooting into me, as I and Wolfgang both tried to stifle sighs of ecstasy. After he had finished shooting his load, he whispered: 'Das was zehr gut, danke!' and he pulled out of me, rolled over and reached for his cigarettes.

As he smoked, he put his arm around me. 'I vas not too rough, nein?' he said.

'No, I liked it, thank you,' I said.

'But you haf not cum,' said Wolfgang. 'You like me to make you shoot.'

'Oh, would you do that?' I said with genuine surprise. I hadn't really expected him to be so considerate, especially after he'd had his fun with me. It was then I knew Wolfgang was someone special.

He lay there smoking and jerking my cock under the bedclothes. Then he finished his cigarette and threw back the sheets, and really went to town. He kissed me, sticking his tongue right down my throat, and vigorously wanked me. As I got near to climax he whispered: 'You vill cum! You vill cum because I have been fucking you, and now I order you to spunk! Spunk fuer die Wehrmacht! For the German army, you vill spunk!'

I shot my load right a across the bedroom. The thought of being made to shoot on the orders of the German army was just too much - I was going to be their hot little bitch, I knew that.

Wolfgang must have read my thoughts, because a few minutes later he whispered to me again: 'You like my comrades in ze next room? You like zem to rape you? I can arrange zis!'

'Oh, yes please!' I said eagerly.

'When do your parents go out?' asked Wolfgang.

'They will be out all day Saturday. They are going to visit my grandparents and my sister. I'll make some excuse not to go with them,' I said, my voice full of excitement.

'Yes, you vill do zis, and me and my comrades, ve vill all haf you. Ve vill keep our uniforms on - you like zat, ja?' said Wolfgang, who clearly knew what I wanted.

'Oh yes, please! I just want to service you all,' I said.

'Ja, you vill be servicing many soldiers in the Wehrmacht. I vill make sure of zat! But you are my Hausfrau - you only go viv uzzer soldiers ven I say so. You are my whore, I vill rent you out to ze Deutsche soldaten.'

The thought of being his 'housewife' and 'whore' and being rented out to German soldiers gave me a big thrill. I was indeed a Jerry-bag, and I loved it. I was going to be their hot little bitch, I knew that.

The following Saturday my parents went to visit my sister and grandparents. I said I didn't feel too well, so stayed at home.

I was laying in my bed reading, when Wolfgang came in followed by his three comrades who slept in the next bedroom. They all had their German army uniforms on, as Wolfgang had promised.

Wolfgang then produced two pairs of handcuffs, made me lay face down, and proceeded to handcuff my hands to the railings of the headboard.

Meanwhile the other three soldiers pulled the bedclothes off me and took my pajamas off. I then saw them lining up to fuck me, fondling their big erections inside their uniform trousers.

First to approach me was Franz, but before climbing on top of me he unbuttoned his flies, took out his big cock, knelt on the bed by my pillow and waved his cock in front of my mouth: 'Suck zis,' he ordered, 'Suck it so it is hard and slippery zen I vill fuck you.'

I sucked on Franz's big cock whilst Wolfgang and the other two soldiers stood watching and wanking. It was difficult giving a blowjob with my hands attached to the headboard, but I did my best.

Then Franz, sporting a rock-hard erection, jumped on top of me and rammed his rod of steel right up my bum. He did it with such sudden force that I yelled out in pain.

'Yes, you are being raped by ze German army!' hissed Franz in my ear as he mercilessly plowed in and out of my arse, 'You are under occupation and must service your conquerors.'

'Yes, sir!' I said, as Franz continued to fuck the living daylights out of me. Soon I felt his hot spunk shooting up inside me, a fountain of pure lust.

'Zat is zehr gut!' cooed Franz in my ear, 'I haf filled the sweinhund mit spunk!'

As soon as Franz rolled off me, Hans took his place, gently easing his cock up my back passage which was now slimy with Franz's cum.

'Good boy,' said Hans in my ear, 'You are a good fuck. I fuck you nice and slow. Mmmm, feel my big soldier cock inside you.'

I moaned with pleasure. Hans was so sensual and seductive, after Franz's brutal rape.

After about 15 minutes, during which Hans bit my ear and my neck as he gently fucked me, he said: 'I am cummin' now. Take my spunk, feel it pumping into you slowly, slowly - ahhhhh, zis feels so goooooood! Lovely fuck!'

Hans kissed my neck as he got off the bed, then Jurgen got on top of me. He was a very tall lad, and his long, slim cock must have been nearly a foot long. As he slid it up my spunky arsehole I felt it filling me right up. Higher and higher it went, till it was rammed up against my prostate, causing me to instantly shoot my load.

'Yes, you like Jurgen's big soldier cock inside you,' he said. 'I've made you cum, haven't I? Now you vill let me fill your stomach vith my hot cum.'

Jurgen pushed his long prick still higher and higher till it felt it was almost in my stomach. Even though I had cum, it felt so satisfying. Then I felt it stiffen inside me and spurt its hot load high into my lower

abdomen. I'd never felt anything so intensely in my life, and I'd been fucked by quite a few men.

Finally Wolfgang climbed on top of me and fucked me. 'You are my little bitch, my whore,' he said. 'Did you like my comrades fucking you? But my cock is best, isn't it?'

'Yes,' I said, 'You are my master, I worship your cock'.

'Yes, I am your big blond Aryan master, and my cock is going to fill you vith my spunk,' he said. 'You dirty little bitch, you haf been fucked by four German soldiers and still you vant more. Vell here it is - take my spunk! Take it, take it, you filthy soldiers' bitch-boy.'

Wolfgang shot his hot load up my arse, and I came again at the same time.

Then the three other soldiers laughed as they walked out of my bedroom. Just before he left, Wolfgang came over to the bed and took the handcuffs off. Then he sneered and said to me: 'Be ready zis afternoon - I am renting out your arse to many soldiers. Your mouth too. You vill make me a lot of money today.'

True to his word, Wolfgang kept showing German soldiers into my bedroom all afternoon. I was fucked senseless, sometimes having to give one soldier a blow-job whilst another fucked my arse. I saw Wolfgang collecting the money as the soldiers paid him to fuck my mouth or my bum.

By the time my parents were due home I'd been used by about 50 German soldiers, and my bum was sore. My jaw ached from all the cocks I had sucked, and my insides were full of German spunk.

Wolfgang showed me all the money he had made.

'You vill come vith me to ze barracks tomorrow, and every day,' he said. 'I vill make a lot more money from you. You vill service ze Wehrmacht - ze soldaten zey need a good mouth and tight bum like yours.'

Thruout the entire Occupation I was fucked daily by many German soldiers, sometimes in the barracks, but often in my own bedroom with my parents in the house. They could not really question why German

soldiers were entering the house and going into the bedroom Wolfgang and I shared together, so I was used as a German army fuck-bag right under the noses of my parents. I'd come down to the dining table barely able to walk, so I'm sure my parents must have known what was going on. They didn't dare say anything in case they were arrested. The Germans ruled the roost and could do as they liked. I loved the fact that I was the German army's plaything, and that my parents couldn't do a thing about it.

When the Liberation came, British soldiers also took advantage of me. The German soldiers told them I was a good fuck and more than willing to service anyone in uniform, and so the British army used me just like the Germans had done.

Before he was shipped back to Germany, Wolfgang came to see me.

'You are my bitch. I vant you to come to Germany vith me. I vill fuck you every day, and rent you out to men in Rostock,' he said. I was so happy.

Wolfgang was shipped out by the British army, but he'd given me money and his address so I could follow him. After about a month I secretly packed up a suitcase and took the ferry to France, then went by train into Germany. Across the Western zones of occupied Germany and into the Soviet Zone. Far north of Berlin, on the Baltic coast, was the town of Rostock.

Wolfgang met me at the station, and took me to his flat. For the next few years we lived there, and had great sex. He brought soldiers and other men into the flat to have sex with me, and made a lot of money out of me. Russian soldiers were the most frequent visitors - half the Red Army in the Rostock area must have fucked me.

By 1949 the German Democratic Republic had been declared, and Wolfgang joined the National People's Army. He was moved to a barracks near Kuhlungsborn, a seaside resort further west along the Baltic coast. National People's Army soldiers, and Red Army soldiers, continued to fuck me in the little one-room flat near the barracks Wolfgang had got for me. Of course Wolfgang was also a frequent visitor, often spending the night with me.

Years later we were still together. Wolfgang was a member of the National Democratic Party of Germany, which contained many ex-Wehrmacht and ex-Nazi Party members. It was part of the coalition National Front which ruled East Germany. I joined the Socialist Unity Party of Germany (the amalgamated Communist Party and Social Democratic Party) and eventually became a People's Deputy in the Volkskammer, the GDR parliament in Berlin, Capital of the GDR (East Berlin). By this time Wolfgang was a Berlin city councillor, for we had moved into a flat in the GDR capital, overlooking the Wall and West Berlin.

By the late 1960s Wolfgang and I were 40 years old, and still together. We enjoyed our life in Berlin. Of course he was no longer my pimp renting me out - that stopped back in the early 1950s. But we were not monogamous. We enjoyed the gay scene of East Berlin, which although not quite as open and wild as that in West Berlin, was still pretty eye opening. We thought nothing of walking hand-in-hand down the Freidrichstrasse, and nobody ever batted an eyelid.

Our favorite pick-up joints were the G bar (pronounced GAY bar) and the nearby Mocca coffee bar, both in Friedrichstrasse near the station. The coffee bar was quite outrageous and got packed to the doors, a seething mass of men all groping each other and jerking each other off. Visitors to East Berlin were amazed when walking by these two establishments, seeing men coming out hand in hand and kissing in the street. Later the authorities clamped down on some of these more outrageous places, and all we were left with were public parks, toilets, more respectable gay venues than the Mocca coffee bar and sad little run-down gay places like the Café Klaus.

However, as part of the East German establishment Wolfgang and I had a privileged and good life together in the GDR, then our world came crashing down with the Wall in 1989. We had mixed feelings about this. As loyal GDR citizens we missed the positive socialist achievements and social security of the regime, and the perks of Party membership, but like everybody else we were fascinated by the decadence and riches of West Berlin which was suddenly opened to us.

We are now old men in our late 70s, still living in Berlin. The novelty of the Wall coming down has worn off, and with unemployment high in the East and the decline in the German economy, many think it was a big mistake to reunite the country. We are living on our pensions, so can't afford many of the luxuries we see in the shops and advertised on TV.

But we do make occasional forays into the gay nitelife of Berlin, which is as wild as ever. Sometimes too wild for two men approaching 80! But we still dress up in our leather gear and with the help of Viagra we have some good times with lots of men once a month or so in the leather bars. Lots of big hairy men frequent these places - perhaps that's why the symbol of Berlin is a bear!

Episode 3 — My German Airman

During the Second World War I owned a farm in Kent. We regularly saw and heard the Luftwaffe coming over on their way to blitz London, and saw the tracers of anti-aircraft fire as the British army tried to shoot them down.

Early one morning after one of these raids I was plowing a field near some woods, when I spotted something caught in a tree. Jumping down from my tractor I went towards the woods to investigate. As I got nearer I could see it was a parachute, and this could only mean one of two things - a Luftwaffe crewman had baled out, or an RAF pilot had been shot down.

I carried a gun in my pocket for situations just such as these, and approached the wood carefully. I took out my gun as I drew close, and looking up in the tree I could clearly see a young German airman clinging to a branch. He seemed to be injured, and trying not very successfully to untangle himself from the parachute and the tree branches.

I stood under the tree and pointed my pistol at him, and told him to throw down any weapons he might have on his person. He must have understood English, for he threw down an automatic, which I picked up and put in my pocket. I asked him to throw down any other weapons, and a knife followed, which I kicked into the bushes.

I couldn't climb the tree whilst holding the gun, and I still wasn't convinced he didn't have some other weapon hidden somewhere. So I shouted to him that I would come and get him down, and went back to the tractor so I could go to the farmhouse and get a ladder.

When I got back with the ladder, he had hardly moved, though he had managed to untangle himself a little bit. With my gun in my hand I positioned the ladder against the tree, and cautiously climbed up to

him. I had retrieved the knife from the bushes, and it proved very useful to cut him free of the parachute. Then I reached out for his hands and told him to try and climb on to my shoulders. I was taking a risk, as he could have had another knife or a gun, but so far he had made no attempt to attack me, and I could see a frightened look in his eyes. Of course this could be dangerous, he might panic at any moment.

Anyway, I got him on my shoulders and carried him down the ladder, placing him on the ground. I examined him, and asked him if he was injured. He said his leg hurt. I had some first aid training, so felt up and down his leg - it didn't appear to be broken. There was no blood, so probably it was just bruised. With my help he managed to stand up, and with me supporting him, he limped to the tractor.

It was still early in the morning, and the farmworkers and land-girls were not yet in the fields. I had already decided this gorgeous looking young German pilot was not going to be handed over to the British authorities if I had anything to do with it. I wanted to keep him for myself!

I got him in the tractor, and we made it back to the farmhouse without anyone seeing us. I lived there on my own since my parents died a few years back, so took him inside, laid him on the sofa and asked him to take down his trousers so I could examine his leg.

As I suspected, there were only some scratches and bruising from where he landed awkwardly in the branches of the tree. I rubbed some ointment on his leg, and as I did so his eyes met mine. He was gay, I knew instantly, and he recognized the look in mine. Perhaps I was rubbing the ointment in too sensually, too gently, but as he looked at me he smiled and said: 'Danke'.

'What's your name?' I asked him, and he said it was Walter.

'Don't worry, I'm not going to hand you over to the authorities. You can live here with me if you like. I could do with some company.' I said.

His English was pretty good, and he understood everything I said.

'You are very kind. I would like that very much,' he said.

'Not that I approve of what you were doing, bombing innocent citizens in London,' I said. 'But I guess our boys are doing just the same to your

cities. Still, that doesn't excuse either of you. You deserve to have been shot down, it might have saved innocent lives.'

I thought I'd better set the record straight right away. I was not a Nazi sympathizer, nor a complete pacifist. I was rather old for the army - in my 40s, but I knew I would have been called up had I not been in what was considered a vital occupation, farming.

'I was only following orders,' said Walter. I didn't drop any bombs, I was just the pilot.'

To me these excuses cut no ice at all. To pilot a bomber was just as bad as actually releasing the bombs, and after the War we all knew what the Nuremburg judges thought of the excuse 'I was just following orders.'

I bandaged his leg up as best I could, and gave him some aspirins to dull the pain. Then I got him a hot drink and something to eat.

'I'll have to hide you away in the daytime,' I said, 'Because the farmworkers and land-girls sometimes come in the farmhouse. But they never go upstairs. Do you think you can manage the stairs?'

He said he could, and with my help I got him up to my bedroom, which had a double bed which once belonged to my parents. I got him undressed and into bed, lending him a pair of my pajamas. He looked so cute snuggled up under the covers, with his fair hair and blue eyes. He was much younger than me, in his late 20s I should imagine. I was getting an erection just looking at him, and imagining what might happen that night when I crawled in bed beside him.

'The bathroom and toilet are along the corridor, but try not to turn on the taps in the daytime, and certainly don't pull the chain in the toilet,' I warned him. 'If the farmworkers hear it they'll know there's someone in the house besides me.'

For the rest of the day I tried hard to concentrate on running the farm, giving orders to the farmworkers and land-girls when they arrived. At lunch-time I managed to sneak upstairs with a meal for Walter, and he was very grateful. By now he had gotten up, and was sitting in a chair reading one of my books. I took some clothes out of my wardrobe, and told him to get dressed - luckily we were about the same size. I had

already put his Luftwaffe uniform in a sack, and planned to burn it that night when the farmworkers and land-girls had gone.

At last the day came to a close, and as the last farmworkers left, I crept upstairs to Walter with a cup of tea and some biscuits. I had locked the farmhouse for the night and drawn the curtains, so I told him it was safe for him to come down if he wanted to.

That evening we sat and talked till about midnight. He came from Leipzig, and had studied English in college. He also loved American and British films, so even knew quite a bit of Anglo-Saxon slang. This became obvious when he suddenly said: 'You like to fuck?'

I was a little taken aback by this direct question, and didn't know quite how to answer.

'Well yes, when I get the chance. But I live here on my own,' I said. I had already told him about my parents dying.

'You have no wife, no girlfriend?' he asked.

'No, have you?' I replied.

'No, but I am only 26. I think you are a little older,' he said.

'Yes, I'm 43, but I've never married. I'm not interested in girls in that way,' I said, feeling I was perhaps being too bold.

'Nor me, my parents are always asking when I will get a girlfriend,' he smiled knowingly. 'They don't know I like men, older men. I went to Berlin once, to some clubs where only men go. I was only 18. It was very interesting. But the Nazis, they don't like these sort of clubs. They close them down. Now it is too dangerous to go with men for sex.'

I had heard that Berlin was pretty wild before the War. Now I knew for sure Walter was gay, and joy of joys, he was into 'older men'.

I decided it was time we got to bed, especially as I had to be up early as usual. But the real reason was I couldn't wait to snuggle in beside Walter. I wasn't sure what would happen the first night, if anything, but I wanted to find out.

We went upstairs, and got undressed. Neither of us bothered with pajamas, we climbed in beside each other naked. By this time both of us had roaring erections, and as I put my arms out to cuddle Walter, he melted in my arms and we kissed passionately. His hard cock was throbbing against my stomach, and mine against his.

After we had cuddled and kissed for a while, he said: 'Barry, I want you to fuck me. Will you do this? I haven't been fucked by a man since I was 18.'

Would I do it? He had to be joking, I was longing to fuck his cute little arse. He rolled over, and I lubricated his bum with Vaseline. I gently pushed my cock into him, and he moaned with pleasure: 'Oh Barry, Barry! I've dreamt about this ever since this man I met in Berlin fucked me.'

We had a marvelous, erotic night of hot passion. I fucked Walter four times, and jerked him off three times. We cuddled and kissed, and woke up with our arms still around each other.

Over the next few weeks we learnt a lot more about each other. Walter had been in Berlin to visit an old schoolfriend, who turned out to be gay. They had never done anything together, but each knew the other had never been interested in girls. The schoolfriend, Klaus, took young Walter to a gay club. They both got off with men, Walter meeting a man in his 30s who took him back to a hotel. That was the one and only time Walter had had sex with a man, or a woman for that matter. He had fantasized about that experience many times in the last 10 years.

He told me how difficult it was for him when he was in the obligatory Hitler Youth with all those gorgeous blond teenage males in uniform, and now in the Luftwaffe sleeping in barracks with all those handsome Aryan men around him, and not being able to do anything. There was some horseplay in the showers, but that was all. Some of the airman talked about homosexuals with disgust, and said they were being rounded up in concentration camps, and that it served the little perverts right if they died there. No wonder Walter and any others who were that way inclined kept quiet about it.

To avert suspicion Walter went along to brothels with the other airmen, and even went into rooms with different girls, but he always made some excuse and paid them off without doing anything. He told the other

airmen he had a girlfriend in Leipzig, and showed them a photo of a girl cousin. It was all a lie, he was 100% gay, and so was I.

I'd had a slightly easier time. My parents had given up asking why I never had a girlfriend, or why I never got married. My stint in the army in the First World War was very short-lived, as the night before I was due to be sent over to France they found me in bed with another soldier. We were both kicked out of the army, and put in prison for the duration.

It was the worst place they could have put two homosexuals if they wanted to reform us, but it suited us well. We were out of the War, and we had plenty of sex in there from straight inmates starved of female company.

We two were fought over by the inmates. The only problem was that I was more active than passive, but in prison I was fucked every day, sometimes by several inmates.

On coming out I resumed my butch active role again, meeting men in public toilets, and occasionally going up to London to visit the secret gay meeting places there in pubs and clubs. It was relatively easy taking someone back to a hotel room, since few people in those days thought there was anything suspicious about two men sharing a room together.

In the air-raids when I stayed in London, I found quite a bit of hanky-panky going on in some of the air-raid shelters. Most of it was between men and women, but I had quite a few encounters in the dark with other men, and on several occasions with British, Canadian, Polish and American military personnel, both in the shelters and outside in dark alleyways during the blackout. All in all, the War had been pretty good to me. Now it had given me Walter, my German airman.

I managed to keep Walter hidden throughout the War. Living on a farm, there was no problem finding enough food to feed him. Rations meant little to us, for I could always manage to hide away sufficient meat and vegetables for us both. Whenever he got ill there was a problem, as I couldn't call a doctor, but using my little medical knowledge I nursed him as best I could. The worst he suffered, after the initial scratches and bruising from the parachute jump, was the occasional cold, and once a sprained ankle when he tripped on the bottom stairs.

We made passionate love every night for the duration. We got more adventurous, having sex all over the farmhouse, in the barn, and even out in the open fields. His English accent became so good, that occasionally we ventured out to the nearby village together, where I introduced him as my cousin, on a few days leave from the RAF. We couldn't do this too often, as fit young men of Walter's age just didn't get that much leave in wartime.

Once we were nearly caught in the barn, when Walter was giving me a blow-job. I was laying back in the hay, and he was just bringing me to a climax when the village policeman shone his torch into the barn.

'Anyone in there?' he asked sternly, and I heard his gun click. Obviously he had drawn his weapon, suspecting a German airman was hiding in the barn.

'It's OK, it's only me,' I said, signaling to Walter to keep quiet. He covered himself with hay and I climbed down the ladder to where Charlie, the village policeman, was standing.

'Oh, sorry Barry, I thought we had a Jerry in here. There were a few shot down around here last night,' he said. 'Never did catch that one who landed in a tree over by the woods a few years ago.'

'I lost a ring today, it belonged to my mother,' I lied. 'I thought it might have come off in here, so I came to look for it.'

Not a very convincing story, and Charlie wasn't very impressed.

'Not much chance of finding it in all this hay. Like looking for a needle in a haystack. You'd stand a slightly better chance in the morning when there's some light,' he said.

'I know, anyway it's probably in the house somewhere,' I lied again. 'But I just thought I'd look up there at the top of the barn before I went to bed. You see, I was working up there this evening, and it was just after that I noticed it missing.'

'Well, hope you find it. Goodnight, Barry, I've got to try to find those Krauts', said Charlie, saluting me as he got on his bicycle and went on his way.

After 10 minutes I climbed back up the ladder, and Walter finished the blow-job. It seemed all the more enjoyable because of nearly being caught by the village policeman, but he knew me well and I doubt if he'd have arrested us even if he had caught us in the act. After all, he thought Walter was my cousin, not a German. However, it would have been acutely embarrassing, and Charlie would have given us both a very stern dressing down, and warned us not to be caught in the act again.

After the War ended, Walter and I continued to live together at the farm. Everyone thought he was my cousin, John, now released from the RAF. We ran the farm together and lived as lovers for over 30 years, till Walter/John sadly died of a heart attack in 1975. He was 58.

I was 75 when he died, and although the sexual side of our relationship subsided as we grew older, we cuddled and kissed right up to the end, and managed sex several times a year. Since he died I have sold the farm and moved to London. I've been with rent-boys a few times, but apart from that I've been on my own. I miss Walter very much, but at my age it won't be long before I join him and we'll be together again. I've had a good life, and Walter has been the best part of it.

SPUNKINALS
(CUMMINALS IN USA)

Everyone's heard of Urinals, the dying breed of male-only toilets which used to stand in the streets of Paris and other cities. In Paris they were called by the charming name of 'pissoires' I believe. Amsterdam had them too, even London had a few. The idea has been revived at Vauxhall bus station I see.

Well, with the death of cottaging in UK and the almost complete absence of glory-holes outside of gay clubs, I think it's time the Spunkinal was introduced as a place where gay men and bisexuals can get quick oral relief. Also those straight men who are not too fussy whether it's by a male or female mouth, or whose wives and girlfriends either won't give head or are no good at it.

Where to place these Spunkinals would be the problem. Obviously they couldn't be in the street where they would shock women and corrupt minors. There would be similar problems with minors in the few remaining public toilets. So the best place would in fact be gay pubs and clubs, and adult cinemas and book stores I guess.

A Spunkinal is basically a specially designed booth with a low seat and glory holes. A window or peep hole at eye-level would be useful so the sucker can see who he is servicing, and vice versa.

Of course this is really going back to the old toilet cubicle with glory-holes, but in this day and age why not be completely open and above board? No need to vandalize public conveniences and risk minors becoming involved. Spunkinals in adult cinemas and bookstores would only be accessible to adults over the age of 18. There is, of course, no reason why women shouldn't make use of Spunkinals to service men, if they feel so inclined.

Spunkinals could be installed in gents' public conveniences if an attendant was present to make sure only adults over the age of consent were allowed in. There is, in fact, a strong case for separate public toilets for minors anyway, and some public parks have introduced them in children's playgrounds.

So here is my story about a Spunkinal installed in an adult male toilet outside a big British Army barracks in London. There is access to the male toilet from inside the barracks, and from the street. Inside the toilet, monitored by an attendant, there are the usual urinals, and the regular cubicles clearly marked as W.C.s.

However, thru another door marked Spunkinals, there are 20 cubicles arranged around the room. You put in a coin and it allows you so much time. This avoids the old problem of guys, who once they get in there, stay all day and refuse to budge. After your time is nearly up a light flashes to warn that you have 5 minutes to finish what you are doing, then the door opens automatically. If nobody is waiting outside, you are then free to insert another coin and continue for another 30 minutes.

So here I am in this marvelous new Spunkinal outside the barracks. I go in and find several strapping young guardsmen in their khaki uniforms waiting for a free cubicle, plus men in suits, builders, college students (over 18 of course, they have been vetted by the attendant and have to give proof of age) etc.

I stand outside a cubicle between two guardsmen. You know which cubicles are going to be vacant first, as a display indicates how long before the door is due to open.

The blond guardsman to my left is first. His cubicle door opens and he goes inside. Five minutes later the door to my right opens, and the red-headed guardsman goes in. I wait impatiently for my cubicle door to open; 3 minutes to go! Let's hope the two guardsmen don't get satisfied before my door opens; after all they each have two glory-holes to service them, one each side.

My door opens, and an old man of about 80 comes out. I pay my one pound for 30 minutes, and dive in. Looking thru the peepholes at various levels I see the red-headed guardsman is standing by the far wall being serviced orally by someone in the cubicle the other side of him. Drat, I had hoped to suck them both off.

Never mind, I look thru the peephole on my right at eye-level when I am sitting down on the low seat, and see the blond guardsman is also sitting, looking in my direction. I bend down to look thru the glory-hole, and see his muscular, tanned and tattooed arms stroking his long circumcised cock, which is rigidly sticking obscenely out of his khaki trousers; he hasn't bothered to pull them down. His bulging tattooed biceps emerging from his rolled up khaki shirt are a real turn-on for me, especially when he sees me looking thru the hole and he flexes his left bicep right in from of it, inviting me to lick it. I kneel down and just before I put my tongue thru, I see he has the words 'SPUNK' and 'RAPE" tattooed on his upper arm muscle. These words are tattooed in thick red letters above and below a red cock which is spurting a big load of cum, outlined in blue. As I put my face right up to the hole and stick my tongue thru to lick this obscene Army tattoo, I feel the warmth of the soldier's flesh and smell Army soap. I start licking thru the big glory-hole, and he whispers: 'That's right, you fuckin' faggot. Worship the power of the Army, worship my muscles. You'll be worshiping another muscle in a minute.'

True to his word, he then stood up and thrust his beautiful cock thru the glory-hole. I heard the command: 'SUCK!' from the other side, and I opened my mouth and took his throbbing member right into it. Instantly I could taste his sweet pre-cum on my tongue, and as I started to suck him I could hear him breathing heavily. He wouldn't take long to shoot, I knew that. 'Oh yes, yes, that's right you dirty little queer! I'm gonna feed you a big load of Army spunk. Get ready, here comes your lunch!'

With that his big cock jerked violently in my mouth as he spewed hot sperm into it and right down my throat. He must have been saving it up

for ages, as he spurted about 8 times, filling my mouth to overflowing. I was almost choking with his thick, sweet, soldier cum!

'Swallow it all down while it's still hot,' I heard him say, as he zipped up and got ready to leave.

As I was still savoring his delicious load and sitting back in my seat, I saw the red-headed soldier the other side was looking thru the glory-hole. He had seen me sucking the other soldier off, and was now looking up at my spunk-covered lips and chin as I strove to swallow the blond soldier's huge load.

He beckoned me close to the hole with his finger and whispered: 'You filthy fuckin' cunt! So you like drinking soldiers' loads do you?'

I nodded, as I swallowed the now thickening last globules of thick spunk the blond soldier had just fed me. 'OK, here's your dessert. On your knees, cock-sucker!' he ordered.

I fell to my knees, and his freckled uncut cock came thru the hole, stiff as a ramrod. The words SPERM FEEDER were tattooed down its length! I gingerly pulled back the foreskin, and saw a big pearl of clear pre-cum oozing from the tip of his cock head. I squeezed more out, then licked it off, cleaning the inside of his foreskin with my tongue. The soldier started moaning: 'Oh, oh, that's right bitch, make me feel GOOD!'

I then took his whole eight inches into my mouth and gave him a long, slow blow-job. His moans got louder and louder as he slowly neared climax. He was in no hurry, he wanted this suck-off to last as long as he could hold out. He kept calling me 'his bitch' and asking me how I liked the taste of his soldier cock. Each time he asked me I took his cock out of my mouth and told him I LOVED it, and that I was just born to service soldiers like him, and other young real men.

'That's fuckin' right, and don't you forget it!', he said. 'Keep sucking, you're my slut bitch and you're gonna get a big feed in a minute. I'm gonna empty my soldier balls right into your faggot mouth!'

Fifteen minutes after I first licked his pre-cum off his cockhead, he finally started to orgasm right in my mouth. It sounds disgusting to see this described in print, but this is what was happening to me and many other queens in that Spunkinal room. The soldier moaned and groaned

as he shot a huge load of his delicious spunky fluids into my mouth. 'I'm thinking of my girlfriend, you faggot, not you!' he said as he came. 'Oh Katie, yeah, drink my sperm! Drink it all down.'

My mouth was filled to overflowing once again with soldier cum. These squaddies were really horny young lads.

As the soldier zipped up, he bent down and said thru the glory-hole: 'How d'ya like the taste of my lust for my girl?'

'It tastes absolutely delicious,' I said, struggling to swallow as I spoke, but spunk was spilling out over my lips.

'Disgusting queers!' he snarled, 'But you serve your purpose when our women won't oblige. That cum is the taste of a real man's lust for his woman, that's why you got such a big load! Drink my baby-juice, and I hope it fuckin' makes you pregnant!'

He exited the Spunkinal, and I noticed on my right a ten inch long monster was protruding thru the hole waiting to be sucked off. I stood up and looked thru the peephole, and could make out the handsome face of a young man. He saw me looking and leant back so I could see his head and shoulders. It was an attractive dark-haired man of about 25 in a city suit, white collar and blue tie. I loved guys in suits, so fell to my knees and instantly smelt his Tommy Hilfiger body lotion as I took his long, thin erect prick into my mouth. It was so long it reached the back of my throat and nearly choked me, and the taste and smell of his Tommy fragrance, with which he'd smothered his 10 inch cock, was overwhelming. It made me crazy with desire for his load, even though I'd just been well fed by two strapping guardsmen.

As I sucked, he moaned and moaned, then said: 'Wish the young bank clerks would learn to do this. You're a bloody good cock-sucker. Get ready for a liquid office lunch. Here it cums....'

With a huge groan his big cock throbbed in my mouth and spurted his hot sperm right down my throat. I pulled away slightly, so the second, third and fourth spurts went right into my mouth where I could taste the flavor of his thick cum on my tongue.'

'How did you like the taste of THAT orgasm?' he asked me as he zipped up.

'It was lovely, thank you sir!' I said, as a cock-sucker always should to his feeder when asked such a question.

'I work in the bank next door,' he said. 'I'm on duty tomorrow morning when we open at 9 a.m.. Be outside before 8.30. I have a job for you to do'.

Wondering what on Earth he meant, I promised to do as he said. Meanwhile there was another cock waiting for me to suck off the other side of me, but I knew my time was nearly up and the red light would be flashing soon. So a quick look thru the peephole to see who it was, and I was amazed to see my 18 year old nephew who I had often lusted after. I don't know if he knew it was his uncle next door, but if not I didn't give him a chance to find out. I dropped to my knees, and sucked that gorgeous teenage cock I had often imagined in my mouth. I couldn't believe my luck; soon my handsome nephew would be depositing his teenage semen in his uncle's mouth, and probably not even realizing it was me.

My thoughts were confirmed when he called out: 'I'm cummin', cocksucker! Drink my teenage load, whoever the fuck you are!' And with that he filled my mouth for the fourth time in less than 30 minutes with hot spunk. His load was really thick and sweet, and I really enjoyed it knowing it was my gorgeous nephew Jason's sperm I was tasting at long last.

'Wanna cum, mate?' he asked, and as the red light was flashing I just put my cock thru, not wanting him to recognize my voice. I heard him spit on his hand, and sensuously and expertly he thrilled me with a quick but efficient hand job which soon had me on the verge of a huge climax. Just as I was about to shoot I felt his lips and wet mouth enclose my cock, and I obscenely fed my teenage nephew's mouth with my hot spunky load. I heard the filthy sod moaning as he tasted my cum, and even though he had already cum himself he was guzzling my sperm down greedily, like he was ravenous for it.

I couldn't resist bending down and looking at his sperm covered lips and chin before I went, and he of course recognized me for the first time. 'Uncle Ray!' he said astonished, then he smiled: 'I've always dreamt of sucking you off, but didn't know you were that way inclined. Thanks for the feed. I'll come round to your flat tomorrow for more, if I may.'

'Of course, Jason, any time, and I look forward to another feed from you,' I said. Such a thoughtful, well-brought up young man; asking his partner if he wants to cum, instead of just rushing off after being satisfied like so many do. Politeness and good manners run in our family.

Next day I was at the bank before they opened. At 8.30 the guy in the suit I had sucked off the day before in the Spunkinal opened a side door and beckoned me in. I followed him into the empty bank and he led me behind the counter.

'You will sit under there and suck me off all morning while I serve customers,' he said. I looked where he pointed, and saw that in front of his chair under the counter by the window where he served customers was a deep, closed in cubby-hole with a little footstool. I climbed in and sat on the footstool, and he then sat down with one leg each side of me. He undid his fly, and fed me his cock.

'You'll have to stay there sucking me off until lunchtime when the other counter clerks leave,' he said. I started sucking him right away, and his cock grew hard and stiff in my mouth. I heard the other counter clerks arrive, men as well as women. I could see a woman's legs beneath a long skirt next to the guy I was sucking. If only she knew what was happening just beneath the counter!

At 9 a.m. customers started arriving, and I just kept servicing my gorgeous young bank clerk as he serviced his customers. He stifled his moans of ecstasy a he came, but even so I heard the woman counter clerk next to him ask him several times if he was OK. Altogether he fed me 10 loads during the morning. I'd never done anything so perverted in my life as suck a bank clerk off as he served customers, without them or his colleagues suspecting a thing. He even pissed in my mouth once, and I had to drink it all, what else could I do? My mouth was at his personal service to use as he wished.

At lunchtime he told the woman next to him to go to lunch, and I heard a man arrive to take her place. I wondered how I was going to get out, as the bank didn't shut for lunch. But my spunk feeder had it all worked out.

'OK, you can come out now, but keep down low so the customers don't see you,' he ordered as he stood up to let me out.

'You little devil, Gary. Has he been there all morning?' said the other bank clerk, who was obviously intrigued. 'Can I borrow him this afternoon?'

'Sure you can. You! Get under there now,' hissed Gary, pointing to a similar cubbyhole next door. 'Enjoy, he's very good,' whispered Gary to his colleague.

So I spent the lunch hour and part of the afternoon sucking off this other guy, who also wore a suit, was 6 foot tall, with a close cropped head, and who had a lovely spunky cock which came another 6 times in my mouth. When they thought no-one was looking, they made me get back to Gary's cubby hole, and I sucked him off another 8 times before the bank closed. When the other counter clerks had gone, Gary and his colleague let me out the side door where I had come in. I was well fed, but dying for the toilet. So I went in the convenience next door, and thought I might as well make use of the Spunkinals while I was in there.

An hour later, after sucking off another uniformed guardsman, a policeman in uniform and several builders and office clerks, I headed home to find my nephew Jason waiting outside my flat to feed me his load, and drink mine.

Life is all go, isn't it? No rest for the wicked!

GAY CRUISE

I saw the holiday advertised in the Gay Press; a two week cruise around the Mediterranean for gay men. It sounded like a lot of fun, so I booked it up.

I arrived at the ship, the Rainbow Queen, and a gorgeous young blond cabin boy, aged about 18, dressed in a smart white nautical uniform showed me to my cabin. I'd booked a single, but was surprised to find a double bed, so I asked him if this was the right cabin.

'Oh yes, sir,' he replied, 'All our cabins have double beds. We want you to enjoy yourself on this cruise, even if you're traveling alone. All the crew are at your complete service, sir.'

He winked at me and groped his crotch, so I could be in no doubt what he meant. I most definitely was going to enjoy this cruise. It was advertised as exclusively for gay men (there was another ship and a separate cruise for gay women). So we could all relax and be ourselves, with no inhibitions, for two glorious weeks. Well, whilst on board ship at any rate.

'What do I have to do if I need service?' I asked.

'It's all in the brochure on your bedside table, sir,' said the cabin boy. 'You just ring this buzzer and one of us will come to attend to your needs. Or you can specify which crew member you wish to attend, and book a time. We're all listed in the brochure, sir.'

Obviously the 'entertainment' promised was going to include some very personal services. The ship appeared to be a floating male brothel, but I soon discovered it was much more than that.

As I studied the program of entertainment and tours in the brochure, and the facilities on board ship, I got more and more excited. Every night there was a cabaret, which included strippers with 'audience participation'. There were interactive game shows 'to get to know your fellow passengers and crew members intimately'. The brochure pulled no punches - there were photos of guys getting fucked/sucked on stage in both the cabaret and the game shows, and crew members were participating. I saw a picture of my blond cabin boy being fucked by a passenger in some game show called 'Chicken Run'. 6 contestants had to find their way thru a maze, from 6 separate starting points. In the middle of the maze was a bed with the cabin boy lying face down with his bare buttocks exposed. A large mirror on the ceiling and video cameras showed all the action, with close-ups of the fucking scene on a big screen, according to the description. The first contestant to get into the 'bedroom' got the prize, the boy's butt. This was just one of many such game shows to be held thruout the cruise.

The on-shore cruises included night time visits to gay bars and clubs, and the daytime tours included visits to gay nudist beaches and cruising areas. There were also the more usual excursions such as city sightseeing, though with the promise of 'handsome couriers' to see to your every need whilst on the boring bus journey from the port to the cities we were visiting. I went on several excursions, and the couriers were positively encouraging everyone to have sex with each other on the buses. They paired up guys, and those who didn't fancy each other were moved around till they found someone they liked to sit next to. The few mainly older guys who couldn't get someone they fancied, got the full attention of the couriers. Nobody was left out. As we passed along country roads thru villages and along city streets, a mass orgy was going on inside the bus. Guys being given blow-jobs, or being fucked in the reclining seats designed to go right back almost horizontal. Curtains could be drawn if you wanted privacy from prying eyes, but this was only really necessary in the city when moving in slow traffic. Gay porno videos were showing in the bus the whole time.

As for facilities on board the ship, there were darkrooms and backrooms of every description: The Barracks (where everyone was given military uniforms to wear), The Golden Shower Room, The Red Handkerchief Room, The Leather Dungeon, Scally Boys' Alley, Skinhead Room, The Bear Pit, etc. I tried out quite a few of these in my two weeks on board.

There was also a gym and swimming pools which proved to be very interesting. I took a quick tour of the ship before lunch, and discovered very good looking coaches and lifeguards in the gym and swimming pools, and saw a lot of sexual activity going on. Guys lifting weights in the gym were being sucked off at the same time, and all the swimming pool changing cubicles had glory holes in them, as did all the public restroom cubicles. Gay porno movies were showing everywhere all around the ship, and some of the crew members were walking around with their flies undone and stiff cocks protruding out of them.

In the dining room at lunch, our cute Moroccan waiter had his smooth golden brown cock out as he served us. Everyone on my table had a good suck, and then he came a big spunky load all over my lunch! I gobbled it up whilst the others at my table looked on enviously, and the Moroccan waiter knelt by my side and jerked me off under the table saying obscenely: 'Yes, eat my thick white Moroccan cum sauce, my friend. You like Kamel's sweet spunk? My sperms taste nice, no?' I shot my load off under the table as he wanked me and talked this absolute filth in his charming broken English.

However I got a bit of a shock at the end of the meal. All meals and most entertainment were included in the price of the cruise, but the waiter handed me a bill for his 'personal services'. This would be added to my credit card bill, along with the drinks, tours, photographs and other extras. I now saw the catch; with all this temptation around, it would be very easy indeed to run up a huge credit card debt in no time! What the heck, I was on holiday, and I was going to enjoy myself.

That night my cabin boy, who's name was Yuri, came in to ask if I needed anything before I retired for the night. I said I could do with some company, and he said he could spare an hour. He came over to me and placed my hand on his crotch thru his white uniform. I could feel his cock growing bigger, and he groped me thru my jeans, pulled me closer and gave me a long French kiss, sticking his tongue right down my throat.

He came from St Petersburg in Russia, he told me, and he loved to be fucked. I didn't need asking twice. He lay face down on my bed, and unzipped the back of his white uniform trousers to expose his cute bubble butt. I was rock hard by this time, and with the aid of some lube (supplied with condoms all around the ship) I was soon right up him.

Before 15 minutes had passed we were both naked in the bed, and I was really getting my oats. He moaned as I came, then he asked if I wanted to suck him off, or if I'd had enough. He looked so cute, I thought I've got to taste his load, and so I sucked him right off. He shot such a lovely, sweet, teenage load of thick cream down my throat I was horny again, and he then sucked me off. I blasted another full load of spunk into his face. He was covered in it, and it was dripping out of his mouth. He licked his lips, got dressed, and went on to his next cabin with my spunk still all over his face. Of course I got another bill, but it was well worth it!

Next day I explored the gym, swimming pool and backrooms on board, and got plenty of good, free sex with other passengers, without any bills to be added to my credit card. Could I stand the pace? At this rate I'd be shagged out within a few days.

At the cabaret that evening, they had a game show called 'Guess Who?' Seven contestants were invited on stage to face seven crew members in their smart sailor uniforms, with their first names clearly emblazoned on their sailor caps. The crew members unzipped their flies, and took out their cocks. Each contestant was allowed to feel and suck each cock in turn. Then the contestants were blindfolded, and made to sit on chairs. One by one each crew member stuck his cock in each of the contestant's mouths, and the game was to guess which cock belonged to which crew member. After they'd sucked a cock, each contestant had to shout out the name of the crew member they thought they'd just sucked. The winner, of course, was the one who guessed most cocks correctly. Tonight the prize went to a Dutch guy named Jan who identified 5 of the 7 cocks correctly. He got to go to bed and spend the entire night with any two of the 7 crew members he chose.

This was followed by a stage show in the main theater, and this included a pop group, male strippers and live sex on stage between 6 crew members. Members of the audience were chosen and invited up to participate. The long-haired lead singer of the pop group was being sucked off by a guy from the audience as he sung his encore: 'Make me Cum', and his band members spunked all over him and the guy who

was kneeling down doing the blow-job. He staggered off stage covered in cum!

The finale was when the strippers, the pop group and 10 crew members invited 20 audience members - the first to get to the stage - to come up and participate in an on-stage orgy. This went on for 30 minutes, with close-ups flashed on to the big screens each side of the stage. DVDs of all this sex action could be bought, and added to your credit card bill.

I had a marvelous two weeks, and came back with a stack of DVDs of myself having sex with loads of gorgeous sailors and cabin boys. This was enough to keep me horny until my next cruise in 6 months time. It took me that long to pay off my credit card bill!

FANTASY ISLAND

This story, unfortunately, is fiction. But I wish there were places like this in London. We are slowly getting there, but nothing quite like this at the moment.

A new club had just opened, and I'd heard and read so many good reports about it I decided to pay a visit. It was the gay sex club to top all similar clubs.

The club was vast, in a converted warehouse. It had three floors above ground level plus a basement. As you went in there was a map of the club on the wall, and you were handed a leaflet with a map and a description of the various areas and facilities the club had to offer.

First of all I sat down in the lobby, before paying my entrance fee, and read my options. For an all-in price I could visit all the areas. The ticket would be valid for 24 hours, and I could come and go as I pleased. The areas listed included Police Station, Army Barracks, Prison Dungeon, College Classroom, In The Navy, Hard Hats/Hard Cocks, Strippers/Sex Shows, Cinema, Dirty Dancing Disco, Sauna, Glory Hole Cubicles, The Public Toilet, Watersports/Golden Showers area, Slaves' Dungeon,

Office Sex, Skinhead Alley, Suck Off Room, Rape Room, Gang Bang Room, etc., etc.

Practically every gay fantasy was catered for, and if you weren't satisfied after all that, there was even a special area where strippers and rent boys plied their trade called the Lust Boxes area. More about that later.

I decided on the all-in 24 hour ticket, and found out that if I paid extra I could hire special clothes and equipment, such as an army or school uniform, whips, handcuffs, sex toys, rubber suit, leathers, etc.

First I wandered into the Army Barracks area, and it really was like walking into a military barracks. Guys dressed as soldiers, some in full uniform, were having sex on bunk beds, whilst others were being abused by soldiers in an area called the Glasshouse (the military jail, known as The Brig in the States). Soon after I walked in two soldiers in uniform came up to me and escorted me out of the barrack room into a toilet. One of them shouted at me: 'No civvies in our barracks, unless you're under arrest. And you ARE under arrest, son, for entering military premises unauthorized!'

The other soldier grabbed hold of my arms from behind and held them behind my back, shouting in my ear: 'You came in here because you want to be gang-raped by big butch soldiers, didn't you? You little faggot.'

If these were guys just pretending to be soldiers, they were very good actors. But the exciting thing was you just didn't know. They looked and sounded like real soldiers, and for all I knew they could well be. For the next 30 minutes or so I had the time of my life as the two soldiers repeatedly raped me anally and orally, and forced me to suck off other soldiers who came in to use the toilet. After 6 of them had cum inside me or all over me, they forced me to sit down in a cubicle and four soldiers pissed all over me, and in my mouth.

After this I still hadn't cum, and was now gagging for more. I hired a schoolboy uniform, as my ordinary clothes were now rather damp, but they even had a wash and dry service, so my clothes would be cleaned and ready to wear when I went home. I wandered off into the College Classroom section, and found myself in an all-male classroom, with

guys sitting at college-type desks dressed in similar uniforms to mine, and a tall, blond male lecturer.

'Sit down, Jones, you're late for class.' he barked as I came thru the door. I sat down near the back of a class in an empty seat. A young dark haired guy aged about 18 next to me smiled and looked down at his crotch, and I saw he was wanking himself off beneath his desk. He then reached out and groped me, and 5 minutes later we were wanking each other under the desks. I looked over to my left and saw the guy at that desk a few feet away had another young guy under the desk sucking him off. College was never like this in my day, I must have gone to the wrong one!

Meanwhile the instructor was drawing a huge penis on the blackboard and explaining that for sexual intercourse it had to be erect and then inserted into an orifice of the other person. He described it in such clinical terms, it was actually quite a turn on.

'The penis can also be inserted into the oral cavity or the anus of a man', he was saying. 'If inserted into the mouth you should savor the consistency and flavor of the ejaculation before swallowing the sperm. Jones, are you paying attention?' he looked at me, but the guy next to me carried on jerking me off under the desk.

'Jones, have you ever had anyone ejaculate in your mouth?' asked the lecturer.

'Yes sir!' I replied truthfully, not saying it was just 15 minutes ago, and more than one person.

'Well you're all adults over 18 so that is legal and to be expected. You are at your peak of sexual attractiveness and sexual desire. Since you are so experienced, Jones, stop jerking off Baker there under the desk and come to the front of the class. You can demonstrate to everyone how to do a blow-job,' said the teacher, unzipping his flies and taking out his long, smooth, circumcised cock.

I walked to the front of the class, my cock still sticking out of my gray flannel trousers, and the instructor ordered me to sit down on a chair in front of him. Standing sideways to the class, so they could see everything, he then told me to open my mouth wide and suck him off. As he fucked my mouth he described to the class what was happening:

'Now you see I've inserted my erect penis into Jones' mouth, and when I push it in it goes right down his throat. Jones, being an expert cock-sucker, knows how to relax and take my huge penis without gagging or choking - something you must all practice. Jones, be careful of your teeth - if you bite my cock or scratch it I'll have to cane you. Just suck slowly, there's a good boy.'

I could see from the corner of my eye all the class were now wanking or even sucking each other off. Sex lessons were never like this in my day, all we learnt about was how bees pollinated flowers and birds hatched eggs, very boring!

Suddenly the instructor's cock grew rigid in my mouth and started to throb. He said to the class: 'I'm about to ejaculate into Jones's mouth; he is bringing me to a climax. Suck my hot semen out, Jones, that's right, suck out all my thick, hot, blond sperm! You know you want to drink it! Drink the lecturer's orgasm, that's right! Enjoy the flavor of my ejaculation.'

With that the instructor started shooting loads of hot, thick, sweet cum in my mouth, so much that it overflowed over my lips, down my chin and dripped on to my blue college blazer.

'Don't worry about that, all sexy college boys have plenty of semen on their uniforms,' said the instructor. 'Now Jones, tell the class how you enjoyed the taste of my orgasm'.

I was embarrassed by this filthy talk, but told the class that the lecturer's orgasm tasted delicious.

'Now in a moment it will be the morning break,' said the instructor, 'And the milk monitors will be in the corridors outside to give you all your college milk - straight from their cocks! There are benches - just sit on them and a milk monitor will come up and feed you his cream. We make sure all boys in this college are well fed!'

We all trooped out of the class, and indeed there was a corridor with benches all along one wall. We sat down in a line, and soon the milk monitors in their college uniforms with their 'Milk Monitor' and 'Cum Prefect' badges came along and stood in front of us. My milk monitor was a young tall red head, and he silently unzipped his fly and took out his big stiff cock covered in freckles. 'I'm going to feed you your daily

milk, open you mouth,' he barked, and as he stuck his funky smelling cock down my throat I tasted his sweet pre-cum and found myself staring at a bush of bright red pubic hair. In a few seconds he shot his thick, sweet load right down my throat and as he pulled out he filled my mouth with more of his delicious milk.

'More milk tomorrow morning,' he said as he zipped up and walked away.

By now I was desperate to cum myself, but still hadn't managed it. It was all very well satisfying other guys, but when was I going to get brought off?

I found myself wandering into the Lust Boxes section by mistake. This consisted of little cubicles with windows in them. In each cubicle was a very handsome rent boy or stripper, and they did everything to seduce me inside. According to the leaflet I'd read in the foyer, you could go into as many of these Lust Boxes as you liked and have a session with as many of the rent boys and strippers/lap dancers as you liked, all free of charge so long as you didn't cum. But if you came you had to pay. I decided I might as well have a bit of fun, I wouldn't cum yet, I'd do that in the next area I planned to visit - Office Sex, because I liked men in suits and ties.

A hunky guy with cropped hair and a thin gold chain around his neck was pouting at me from one of the Lust Boxes, and he reeked of some expensive fragrance for men which was very seductive. I couldn't resist, I opened the door and got into the cubicle with him. The warmth of his naked body and the smell of his fragrance overwhelmed me. As soon as I entered he grabbed hold of my cock, which was already rock hard, and started rubbing baby oil into it. At the same time he kissed me, with his tongue deep inside my mouth.

I was already on the verge of cumming, but I tried to stop myself. He withdrew his tongue from my mouth and said: 'Don't resist, it's useless - I've got complete control, I'm gonna make you cum. Give in, you love my fragrance don't you? It's called "Surrender"'. No-one can resist it. Go on, lick my sexy neck, lick all around my lust-chain, it'll make you cum!'

I'd never heard a gold neck chain called that before, but it seemed appropriate — the glint of gold against his tanned, smooth skin was so

seductive it filled me with pure lust, and as my tongue came into contact with the fragrant, tasty, warm flesh of his smooth neck I knew he had me. I was starting to cum!

'That's right, cum for Jason. Just relax and shoot, enjoy my sexy body. Lust for Jason! You're cummin, cummin, cummin. That's right, shoot your load for Jason! You enjoyed that, didn't you?'

I had to admit it was the best hand-job I'd had in years, and I not only paid him but gave him a tip it was so good.

I then went to the cafe and had a coffee, then left to do some shopping. But I would be back within a few hours to take advantage of my 24 hour ticket and to explore some of the other areas of this fantastic club where all fantasies were fulfilled. There was something for everyone here, no matter what you were into, what you looked like, or how old you were.

I arrived back at the club about 8 hours later, all ready for another session on the same 24-hour ticket. This time I headed for the In The Navy section on the second floor. They handed me a sailor's uniform to change into, and as I walked in the decor was got up like the inside of a Navy ship, with sailors, officers and cadets all over the place, up to all sorts of antics. I'd walked in on a mass orgy of sex.

I opened a cabin door marked 'Cadets' Training Room' and found guys in cadet uniform sucking off officers, or being fucked by them up the arse.

'Hello sailor!' said a guy in officer's uniform with his cock pounding in and out of a cadet's backside like an old steam shovel. 'I'm breaking this cutie's arse in for the Navy, why don't you break in his cute little mouth, I reckon he could use a nice hot load of seaman's semen, couldn't you son?'

'Yes sir!' said the cadet, who was bent over as he was being fucked, and who was already reaching for my trousers to get my stiffening cock out. I moved closer, and within seconds his warm, wet mouth engulfed my erect cock, and started sucking me off.

'It's great training young men to serve the Navy, isn't it sailor?' said the officer fucking the guy's other end, 'I'm gonna fill his arse full of spunk in a minute. Is he bringing you off too?'

'Yes sir,' I said, 'I don't think I can hold back much longer, he looks so cute in that cadet uniform, and his mouth is so soft and silky; he's about to suck all the cum out of me.'

'Let's fill him at both ends, sailor,' said the officer, 'One, two, three; take this double load of Navy spunk, cadet! Swallow that nice sailor's load, swallow it all down while I pump my load up your arse!'

I could hear the cadet whimpering as he struggled to swallow my load which was spurting out of my throbbing cock and down his throat in jet after jet of pure lust. I couldn't stop for what seemed like ages. But the cadet swallowed the whole lot whilst taking the officer's load at the same time. As the officer pulled out, the cadet stood up and licked some of my spunk off his lips, then turned half round and saluted us both: 'Thank you sir for breaking me in,' he said to the officer who was now zipping up his fly, then the cadet turned to me and saluted again: 'Thank you sailor for feeding me your delicious cream. Now I'm ready to serve the Navy any time I'm needed.'

With that he staggered away. He could hardly walk because the officer's cock had been so big up his tight little bum. I left the cabin and went out of the In The Navy section, changing back into my own clothes. I thought I'd better have a break from sex as I'd just cum, so headed for the Dirty Dancing Disco. If I thought this would be a sex-free zone I was mistaken, however all I could do at the moment was sit and watch, I was too drained to participate.

I'd never seen such a depraved dance floor. Half naked men were supposedly dancing to sexy music, but I'd never seen a dance floor quite like this even in a raunchy gay club before. As they danced guys were jacking each other off; there was spunk all over the dance floor. Other guys were even crawling on the floor licking it up! A big sign above the dance floor read: 'Cum Dancing', that certainly described what I witnessed, but was nothing like the old BBC TV progam 'Come Dancing'!

Two guys were dancing, one with his back to the other, in a slow sensuous dance, moving slowly around the dance floor. As they passed

me I could see the one behind had his cock right up the other one's arse, and was slowly fucking him as they danced.

Another couple were passionately kissing with their tongues down each other's throats as they ground their hips sensuously together. They were half naked, and their bodies glistened with sweat. I was getting turned on just watching them. As I looked an older guy who had been licking cum off the dance floor, crawled over to them, and prized them slightly apart. I could then see the two dancers had their cocks out, pressed against each other. The guy who had crawled over to them got hold of their cocks and put them both in his mouth at the same time. The dancers carried on kissing and gyrating their hips in time to the sexy music, and then started to moan in ecstasy as they neared their climaxes.

'Oh yeah, taste our young lust for each other, you dirty old man!' said the blond one on the left as he shot his load right into the mouth of the guy kneeling on the floor between them.

At the same time the dark haired one let out a loud moan as he too came in the old guy's mouth: 'Yeah, the filthy old cunt's drinking our orgasms, both of them! Oh God, I can't stop cummin!'

'Neither can I,' said the blond one, 'He's got no teeth, so gives a great blow-job. Let's feed him good! Swallow all our young cum, you disgusting old man!'

'Yeah, oh yeah, this feels so good!' said the dark haired dancer, 'I can feel your spunk swimming around my spurting cock in his sucking mouth; he's milking us both dry! He loves the taste of our loads!'

As the young guys finished cumming, the guy kneeling down, who must have been in his 60s, stood up on shaky legs, his mouth, lips and chin were dripping with thick hot spunk. He swallowed the last drops and licked his lips, and thanked the two dirty dancers: 'Two different flavors of spunk, they made a delicious cum cocktail! You two really got turned on by each other, thank you for letting me drink all the spunk released by your lust for each other! I don't usually get men going like that. I haven't drunk spunky loads like that for 20 years!'

'That's because we're young, good-looking and really hot for each other,' said the blond dancer. 'No offense grandpa, but I'd never have

cum like that if it was just you sucking me off. But you're gumsy mouth with no teeth does give a great blow-job, mate!'

'Neither would I have cum that much just for you, old man,' said the dark-haired one. 'You're OK for your age, pretty sexy, but it was this young blond Adonis who got me really spunking, and you got the double reward!'

'Oh God yes, thank you! You really filled my belly with two good loads of delicious, tasty sperm. Yours was real funky and sweet' he said to the dark haired dancer, and then turned to the blond one: 'And yours was really thick with a taste of almond! Look, you've made me cum in my jeans!'

The two dancers looked down and laughed as they saw a slimy wet patch on the old guy's jeans at the top of his right thigh as he stood up. The blond dancer rubbed his fingers gently over the slimy spunky patch, and then put his fingers in his dark haired dancing partner's mouth: 'Here, taste his spunk,' he said, and the dark haired guy licked his fingers.

'Oh God, I got to have more of that!' he said, and a moment later HE was on his knees, licking all the spunk off the patch in the old guy's jeans, and sucking it dry! Never had I seen such debauchery, and I now had a raving hard-on! I was turned on and ready for some action again.

I didn't have to wait long. I stood up and walked over to where a tall, dark haired guy in a sexy, tight, white tank-top showing off his glistening six-pack and writhing waist was sucking off a young redhead standing on a bench at the side of the dance floor. I stood and watched, with my cock out and wanking, and I heard the redhead moan as he closed his eyes in ecstasy and shot his big spunky load in the other guy's mouth. They had both seen me watching, and beckoned me closer.

The guy doing the blow-job, turned around, and I could then see on the front of his tank-top across his chest in black letters were the words: 'Feelthy Frenchman'. He came over to me, reeking of some erotic French scent, put his sensuous, muscular arms around me and I melted into them, breathing in his scent and feeling his oily, muscular, writhing manly body against mine as we slowly moved on to the dance floor in time to the music.

'Kiss me, suck me, drink my cum' sung the guy on the record, as the Frenchman stared right into my eyes and ground his groin right into mine. I thought I was going to faint, then he moved his spunky lips closer to mine. Closer, closer, until I could now smell the redhead's cum in the Frenchman's mouth. He hadn't swallowed it, and I realized that he was about to kiss me. He opened his lips and I could see his mouth full to overflowing with thick white spunk. I put my head back and just gave in to pure lust. Resting against his muscular arms around my neck, I drank in his French scent as his sensuous, spunky lips made contact with my own lips. I opened my mouth, and his spunk-covered tongue entered. Seconds later the spunky contents of his mouth, the redhead's hot load which the Frenchman had just sucked out of his cock, was oh so slowly transferred into my mouth in thick, gobs of cum mixed with the French guy's spit. It was so dirty, but so fucking erotic!

I was in a daze, literally dizzy with pure lust, as the Frenchman continued to gyrate his hips and move us around the dance floor, never taking his lips off mine or his tongue from my now spunk-filled mouth. We cum-kissed or snowballed like this for what seemed like an eternity, then he slowly moved his head back and I swallowed the redhead's load which the Frenchman had given me.

'Yes, you like ze feelthy French kiss I give you? Eez deesgusting, no?' he said in a delightful French accent, 'Dreenk zat guy's sperms - and I make you cum.' He put my cock back inside my underpants as we were dancing, then he inserted his own cock thru my fly and right into my briefs. Our cocks were rubbing together inside my tight underwear, and I could feel his slimy pre-cum as he prepare to shoot.

'Relax, enjoy zees feelth,' he said, and his lips, still tasting of the redhead's spunk, closed on mine as he French-kissed me again, grinding his groin right into mine. Suddenly I felt hot spurts of his spunk shooting inside my underpants and all over my cock. He was filling my briefs with his cum!

Still he kept gyrating as we danced, and he kept on kissing me till I could hold back no longer. For the second time that evening I let go my load, and with my tight briefs full of the Frenchman's cummy cock and his big slimy load, my spunk-covered cock started shooting my own sperm, until I thought I would faint. My briefs were now soggy with a mixture of my own spunk and the Frenchman's, and he slowly pulled his lips away. By now the redhead had gotten down from the bench and was kneeling on the floor between us.

'Leek out our spunks from hees briefs,' said the Frenchman. 'Clean hees Calvin Kleins of our cum!'

The Frenchman pulled down my jeans, and exposed my spunk-filled Calvin's. Then he guided the redhead's tongue into the fly opening to lick out some of the spunk.

'Now clean zem properly; leek all ze spunks off ze Calvins,' said the Frenchman as he rolled down the elastic waistband, so the redhead could lick out all the Frenchman's spunk mixed with my own inside my underpants.

Cleaned up by the redhead, who licked his lips with satisfaction and crawled back to the bench to sit down, I pulled up my jeans and headed for the exit. I reckoned I had had my money's worth for today, but I'd be back for more in a few days. There were so many areas of this Fantasy Island still to explore.

As I headed for the exit from the Disco, the Frenchman caught up with me, grabbed me from behind and stuck his tongue in my ear, before whispering: 'You cum back again for more feelthy dirty dancing, yes? Next time I dreenk some nice hot piss from a nice young man and I speet it in your mouth as we dance. Tomorrow night, yes?' I nodded, and turned to give him a kiss. He pressed a card into my hand as I left.

In the foyer I looked at it, and it had his address, phone numbers and email. On the card was a drawing of the French guy, who called himself 'Yves de la Orgasm' and underneath was written: 'Feelthy Frenchman' as on his tank-top. But it was the little erotic drawing of Yves' face which I liked most; his long, lanky dark hair hanging down sensuously around his handsome features, his mouth half open, and full of spunk, which was dripping out, as though he was just about to cum-kiss me again!

I had wet dreams about him all night! I couldn't wait to go back to Fantasy Island again the next day.

I was back in my newly found gay club, Fantasy Island, putting my 24-hour ticket carefully away. I decided to explore some areas I'd never visited in this huge emporium, and found myself in the Watersports/ Golden Showers section. They offered me a rubber suit to put on as I entered, but I said I was just going to watch.

In the middle of the room was a metal trough, in fact a huge urinal, and guys dressed either in rubber suits or naked were lying in it and being pissed over. This wasn't really my scene, but they were obviously enjoying it.

I passed thru this room into the Recycled Beer Bar. This was a real eye-opener. It looked like an ordinary bar, but there were no pumps for draft beer and no bottles either. All there were on the shelves behind the bar counter were empty beer glasses.

Guys were sitting on stools, and at tables around the bar, sipping what looked like beer. The bar counter was made of clear glass and ran from one end of the room to the other, and there were as many barmen as customers. I then realized what was happening; the ones this side of the bar, the customers, were the 'takers', the barmen the other side of the bar were the 'givers'.

I watched as a middle-aged man approached the bar towards where a tall good-looking guy with bleached blond hair was standing, empty beer glass in hand, behind the bar counter as though about to pull a pint. The middle-aged man sat down on a stool facing him, and the blond 'barman' held the empty pint beer glass down near his crotch, unzipped his fly, took out his cock and began pissing into the glass. All this could be clearly seen thru the clear glass of the bar. When the glass was full to overflowing with his steaming piss, he lifted it up and placed it on the bar counter.

Eagerly the middle-aged man handed over some money, grabbed hold of the glass and started sipping the frothy, steaming 'recycled beer'. The blond guy zipped up again, watched the man enjoying the drink he had just given him for a few seconds, pocketed the money then turned and exited the room thru a door behind the bar.

This was a great idea. If you liked drinking 'recycled Beer' it could be bought here from the barman of your choice for just a little more than a pint of ordinary beer in any gay bar. If, however, you wanted a piss and were short of a little cash, all you had to do was enter from the bar side of the room, find a willing customer, and Hey Presto, after you'd relieved yourself into an empty beer glass you walked off with cash. Provided you drank plenty of regular beer, water or some other liquid, I imagine you could make quite a bit of money in a few hours.

I made a mental note to find the bar side entrance to this room when I needed the toilet, took one last look at all the dirty old men (and some young ones) drinking their 'recycled beer', then turned and left the Watersports area and headed for the Rape Room and the Gang Bang Room on the same floor.

These too were divided into two sections, one for Rapists and one for their Victims. I decided to be bold and participate this time, so I walked thru the door marked Victims which led into the Rape Room.

As I entered the first thing I saw on the wall was a military-looking sign which read: 'Prisoner of War Camp, Rape Room #1'. Around the room were strange pieces of equipment, all labeled: Rape Rack, Rape Horse, Rape Bed, Oral Rape chair, Spit-Roast Rack, etc.

Men were strapped on to or into these pieces of equipment and were being fucked, or raped, anally or orally. Some of the rapists were dressed in leather gear, some were bollock naked, and others were dressed in military or police uniforms.

As I stood there watching, a big young muscle-bound guy in a tight tee-shirt and skin-tight jeans approached me from the Rapists' side of the room. I could see his pecs and muscles, even his six-pack, rippling thru his white tee-shirt, which had the word 'RAPIST' printed on it in big black letters.

He came up to me, sneered and pushed me over to one of the Rape Racks.

'Put your fuckin' hands up above your head, against the Rack, you fuckin' cunt!' he shouted. I instinctively obeyed, my cock already growing stiff inside my jeans at the thought of being brutally raped by this big butch Adonis. As I put my arms up against the Rack, he attached some leather straps to hold them firmly in place, and then he did the same to my ankles. I was now strapped to the Rack, which was tilted slightly forward. Behind the Rack was a full-length mirror so I could see everything that was happening to me. A mirror on the ceiling gave another view. In fact there were mirrors all around the well-lit room so I could see what was happening to me and all the other victims.

'Know where you are, son?' said my tormenter. I thought I'd better play along with the game.

'N… n… no sir!' I said.

'You're in a fuckin' Rape Camp, son,' whispered the guy into my right ear, and as he pushed himself close up against me I could feel his huge hard cock thru his tight jeans pressing up against me. He put his big muscular arms around me and pulled my torso away from the Rack as far as the straps would allow.

'We are the victors in this civil war, and you are our spoils, son. You've been brought here to give pleasure to your new masters. Get ready to be raped, boy! I'm gonna ram my big cock up your arse and turn you into a pussy-boy. Aren't you excited? A real man is going to make you his bitch!' he said, as he unbuckled my belt and pulled my jeans and underpants down very roughly.

In the mirrors I saw him unzip his fly and take out his huge, stiff cock. He then took some lube and greased up his weapon, then greased up my hole, sticking his fingers right inside and saying in my ear: 'Open up for me, son. I'm gonna break your arse in, then you're going into the Gang Bang Room next door and all the young men in the village are going to rape you! You'll be our pussy-boy.'

With that he took his fingers out of my arse, and seconds later I felt his huge cock head probing the tight entrance of my hole.

'I said open up for your master, pussy-boy!' he screamed in my ear, and I relaxed my anal muscles. A moment later his huge cock was being rammed right up my arse, till I yelled in pain.

'That's right, shout all you like. You'll soon get used to it once I've broken your arse in, then you'll love it; you'll beg for more like the slut bitch you are!' he said as he pounded my arse.

All around me men were screaming as they were being raped, but gradually these screams subsided and became whimpers and then grunts of contentment. The men, the victims, were all being turned into subservient 'comfort men' for their masters, and I felt the same thing happening to me.

My cries and screams were turning into whimpers as I got used to the big cock up my arse, and got familiar with the masculine smell of my rapist.

He whispered in my ear again: 'Yes, you're beginning to enjoy it now, aren't you pussy-boy? You're not a man any more, you're my fuckin' bitch. You're arse is better than my girl's cunt, and I'm gonna fuck you till I make you pregnant. Yes, you'd like that wouldn't you; to have my baby! Well I'm gonna shoot my baby-juice right into you any minute now, and you just might get pregnant. Submit! Submit to me and tell me what you want, pussy-boy!'

I was now moaning with pleasure. I couldn't help myself: 'I submit, I submit! You're the man, you're my master! Please fuck me some more, pump your spunk into me! Please fill me with your cum!' I found myself shouting out these words.

'Yes, you'll get my spunk all right, right now! Here it cums! Aaaaaghh! Urrgggghhh! Urrggghhh!!! Aaaagghh! Yeah! Oh, yeah! I'm pumpin' you full of hot cum, pussy-boy! You're a good fuck, I think I'll take you for one of my regular fuck boys!'

He pulled out, and eventually unstrapped me. I could hardly walk, so staggered to a bed in the Rest Area, where victims were allowed to recover from their ordeal.

After 20 minutes, a guy dressed in U.S. Marine uniform approached me, grabbed me roughly from the bed, and made me stand in front of him. I was sure he was a real marine, possibly from the American Embassy barracks nearby. He stood very close to me with his handsome blond features and cold blue eyes staring straight into mine, his clean-cut cropped hair ending in a neat line around the nape of his smooth neck, and his smooth, tattooed bulging biceps protruding from his light khaki shirt-sleeved shirt. I could feel his hot breath on my face, smell its minty aroma from the gum he was arrogantly chewing, and I could also smell the clean, sexy, soapy odor of All-American, clean-cut, blond, blue-eyed Marine! My cock grew rock solid inside my jeans as he silently opened his lips and spat a wad of spit, gorgeous USMC spit, right into my face and mouth.

'This way, cunt-face!' he barked in an American accent, and I knew this had to be the real thing. He was a real, serving American Marine. If I had any doubts, he quickly dispelled them.

'I've just come back from the front line. We raped thousands of guys on the battlefield, and now it's your turn, son! You're gonna be gang

raped, that's what we do to prisoners of war. That will teach you who's the master race now!'

He took me into the Gang Bang Room, and the sights I saw there were unbelievable. There were similar Rape Racks, etc., but in here long lines of men were waiting to gang-rape each victim strapped to the Racks. Some were dressed casual, some naked, some in leathers, and some in military uniform like the one who had hold of me roughly by my arms. Some were even in suits, but every one of them was a rapist.

I was taken to a piece of equipment in the center of the room and strapped on to it horizontally face-upwards with my back against the leather of the Rape Horse. Again my arms and legs were strapped to the equipment, and there were mirrors on the ceiling. My head was raised by a tilted leather cushion, so I could see the line of men already waiting to gang-rape me. First in line was the Marine, who took out his smooth circumcised cock as a guy dressed head-to-toe in leather greased up my arse with lube. 'He's ready for you now, Corporal!' he said to the Marine, who quickly approached the Rape Horse and rammed his cock right up my arse, showing no mercy.

As he raped me, he bent down low over me and spat in my face again. 'Open your fuckin' mouth!' he ordered, and as I did so he let loose a great gob of spit and his chewing gum right into my mouth. 'Now say thank you for the gum I've given you, gum soaked in my Marine spit,' he said.

'Thank you sir!' I said, and began chewing on the gum as he smiled and continued fucking me.

'Soon you'll submit, you'll be unable to resist, you'll beg me for more!' he sneered. I felt myself drawn to his smooth neck with the sharp cropped blond hairline showing beneath his white Marine cap. He moved nearer and nearer till I could feel the warmth of his flesh, smell his after-shave and that soapy clean Marine smell again. I couldn't help myself, I stuck out my tongue and tried to lick his neck. I couldn't reach it, but he moved nearer, still fucking me, and at last my tongue made contact with his neck. It tasted delicious; the clean tang of All-American Marine! I was overcome with pure lust and I bit into his neck, giving him a love bite. He then bit my neck very hard indeed. 'I've left my mark on you now; that means you're my fuckin' bitch!' he said.

Still fucking me, and getting closer and closer to climax, he turned his head so his eyes looked directly into mine, put his head nearer until our lips were almost touching. I couldn't resist any longer, I lifted my head off the leather cushion and kissed him full on the lips.

He pulled away after a few seconds and shouted to the other men in line behind him. 'Look, he's kissing me! This fuckin' slut is enjoying being raped! Watch this!'

With that he bent over me again, and we were into a passionate snog, with his tongue right down my throat. The leather guy then came and unstrapped my arms, and I flung them around the Marine's neck and shoulders and hugged him close to me as we kissed. As he drew away I said: 'Oh thank you, sir, thank you for raping me! I love you, I worship you, I'm your bitch!'

He sneered and said: 'You're damn right you are! He's fully broken in, guys; he's our willing fuck-boy now! Grab all the ass you want, just let me finish off!'

With that he started snogging me again, then drew back and screamed as he pumped me full of his hot Marine orgasm. I felt my bowels swelling up with spunk, he shot so much into me.

Then he pulled out, gently bent down and kissed me on the lips and said: 'See you again, honey! Have your sweet ass lubed up and waiting for your Marine daddy's big cock!'

Before I could recover, the leather guy, who was tall and slim, clean shaven with dark brown hair protruding from beneath his leather cap, rammed his cock up my arse.

He didn't bend over me at all, just fucked me as though I were a piece of meat. After a few minutes he shot his wad up me, zipped up and moved off. He had hardly looked at me at all, I felt so humiliated.

Next up was a sailor, or someone dressed as one. He smiled at me as he stuck his cock right into my arse. He did bend over me and smiled into my face: 'Hi, I'm Able-Seaman Jason King. You're cute, baby! I'm gonna shoot a big load of spunk right inside your belly!' His cock was long enough to reach up into my belly, or so it seemed.

I guess these guys had already been turned on by the Marine fucking me, as they were shooting so quickly. The sailor quickly unloaded his big wad high up into me. His sexy smell had made me dizzy, but soon it was replaced by the familiar tang of Tommy Hilfiger After Shave as a young city stockbroker type in a pin-stripe suit unzipped his fly and started fucking me. I knew that smell, and as he leaned over and kissed me, I recognized my boss from work! His Tommy After Shave was so strong I nearly passed out. I was filled with lust, as he sensuously stuck his tongue right down my throat, then pulled away and said into my ear: 'Oh Gary, baby, I've wanted to rape you ever since you first came into my office for the job interview, all young and innocent and fresh from school! I'm cummin' just for you, take my cum, it's all for you, baby, all for you. My wife craves my load and I've given her two kids, but this load of spunk is especially for you, baby. Enjoy!'

With that he shot his load into my arse, pulled out, and said: 'Report to my office twice a day, I want more of that. I'll unload my sweet spunk right down your throat at work tomorrow morning whilst Miss Simpson goes for her coffee break.' Miss Simpson was his aged spinster personal assistant.

I was so excited at the idea of having regular sex with my handsome boss in his office just a few feet from Miss Simpson and all the office girls.

It was utterly depraved! In actual fact he made me crawl under his desk in the days to come, and I was sucking him off and drinking his spunk whilst Miss Simpson was taking shorthand notes blissfully unaware of what was going on just inches away the other side of the closed-off desk.

Though she did say: 'Are you all right, Mr Johnson?' when he groaned as he shot his big spunky load into my mouth. I had to stifle my moans of pleasure as I swallowed his deliciously sweet and thick slimy load of cum!

Back in the Gang Bang Room, the next guy quickly took Mr Johnson's place. In all 20 guys raped me in the space of 45 minutes. My arse was sore by then, and finally they unstrapped my legs and I had to be carried by two of the rapists to the rest area. But I couldn't rest; I had so much spunk up my arse, I had to rush to the toilet area and let it all out. It acted like an enema, and I was on the seat for 15 minutes.

Feeling thoroughly exhausted and drained, I then lay on a bed in the rest area for half an hour. Finally I staggered up, and headed towards the Glory Hole area. I wanted to cum, and I thought this would be the best bet for a quickie. I was too exhausted to do much else.

The Glory Hole area, like the others, was divided into givers and takers. This time I went into the active side. The walls were glass so you could see who was the other side. The guys waiting to suck were sitting on stools in front of the Glory Holes. I walked up the line, and chose a Glory Hole behind which was a teenage boy, couldn't have been more than 19, with dyed green hair sticking up in spikes. He had a studded leather belt around his neck with the word 'Pig boy' written on it. He wore a torn punk-style tee-shirt and torn jeans covered in spunk stains. It looked as if the whole bar had spunked over him; there were also spunk stains on his tee-shirt, and there appeared to be dried spunk in his hair and on his face. I shoved my hard cock thru the hole, and immediately felt his silky soft lips, tongue and mouth enclose over the head and begin their gentle sucking.

Faster and faster he went, and I could see the lust in his eyes as they glazed over. He looked up into my eyes as he sucked me, greedy for my spunk! He pulled away briefly and shouted out: 'Feed me, feed me, feed me your load!' then started sucking me again, still looking into my eyes. I stared back into his and gave him what he craved. I let go my cum into his eagerly sucking mouth. It was like feeding a baby; he sucked and gurgled contentedly as I spurted my hot milk into his eager mouth. My cream was overflowing from his mouth over his lips and chin, but he drained me dry. Thoroughly exhausted I pulled out of the glory hole and zipped up, and saw him lick my spunk off his lips and chin. As I moved away the Marine who had raped me used the same glory hole and the punk's mouth, and I stood and watched him take a huge load from the Marine who screamed as he came: 'Drink U.S. Marine Sperm, you cunt-faced punk!'

That was enough for one day. Perhaps I'd feel ready for another session tomorrow. I went home feeling sore at the back but thoroughly contented.

I looked at the passengers in the Tube train. If only they knew where I'd been and what I'd just done a few feet above them. What was still going on now. They had no idea of the debauchery going on behind those walls up on the surface. An old lady looked at me and smiled. I recognized her as my old Sunday school teacher.

'Hallo, Gary, how are you? You look tired. Been working hard?' she asked me.

'Yes, Mrs Peters, I've been worked very hard today. I was under 20 men and I had my work cut out to please them all.' I said wickedly, knowing she wouldn't pick up on the double-meanings.

'That's right, always do your best, and God will reward you,' she smiled, clutching her Bible, and I felt ashamed that I had teased her so. 'You always were a good boy, God Bless!' she said as she got up and left the carriage.

I felt a little guilty, but then spotted a Roman Catholic priest further down the car. He was pretending to be playing with his rosary whilst stroking his hard cock thru his black robes. The priest was leering at a young lad, who couldn't have been more than 11, sitting with his mother on the seat opposite. The dirty old fucker! At least I went with consenting adults, yet he was a religious man of the cloth, supposed to be celibate.

I left the carriage feeling much better about myself. After all, I hadn't done anyone any harm. I was definitely going back to the club tomorrow night, and I also had two sex sessions lined up in Mr Johnson's office at work beforehand. Life was good!

A few days later I was back in my favorite gay raunch club. This time I headed straight for the stage area, where two strippers were due to appear. It was their name which attracted me, 'The Spunky Kid and His Cum Slut', plus reports I'd heard about their act. I got a spot right down the front, and two good-looking guys with well-toned muscles (not over-developed) showing thru their tight t-shirts appeared. They wore tight leather jeans, with their big cocks clearly visible as bulges in the stretched leather. One was a redhead, and the other was blond. They were both in their mid-20s. The redhead had the words: 'Spunk Feeder' printed on his t-shirt, and the blond had 'Cum Drinker' written on his. This looked like an entertaining act, more of a 'live' sex show than just a double strip act.

They went thru the usual sort of strip routine to a backing tape, ending up with their muscular, naked, writhing bodies glistening with baby oil. I and other members of the audience had been invited to smear this all over them as they jumped down amongst the crowd.

Now they were back on stage, and the blond Cum Drinker was kneeling before the redheaded Spunk Feeder and sucking him off. I wondered how far they would go, and as the audience cheered and urged them on, the redhead started moaning and groaning as he neared his climax.

'I'm gonna cum, I'm gonna feed you my big spunky load, here it cums, oh, oh, oh yeah!', sighed the redhead as his big cock quivered half-an-inch from the blond's open mouth ready to receive his creamy meal. 'Aaagggh! Urrrgh! Oooh! Yeah! Show the guys how you love me feeding you my cum!'

We watched as spurt after spurt of thick, hot sperm shot from the redhead's throbbing cock straight into the blond's eager mouth. Some of the spunk went over his face, and in his eyes. There was so much of it, that very soon the blond stripper's face was covered in thick spunk, and his mouth was full to overflowing, it was running over his lips and down his chin.

The redhead pulled me and another guy on to the stage, and told the other guy to lick the spunk off the blond stripper's face. Then he told me to kiss the blond stripper, and soon we were in a passionate, lustful, spunky kiss. The blond leant over me, opened his mouth and let all the redhead's spunk dribble from his mouth into mine, then stuck his spunky tongue right down my throat and we kissed long and hard, savoring the taste of the redheaded stripper's sweet cum.

As we kissed, the audience were egging us on, and I felt the redhead come up behind me and start jerking me off with baby oil.

'Watch, I'm gonna make him cum,' he said to the audience. To me he said: 'How d'you like the taste of my spunk? Now swallow it, all of it. That's right. Now face the audience, I'm gonna make you shoot all over them!'

With the blond still kissing me and now grabbing hold of my balls, the redhead brought me to my climax, and pointing my cock at the audience he ordered me to spunk.

The blond stopped kissing me and told me to look down at the audience, and I couldn't believe what I saw: a young lad of about 18 was standing right beneath me with his mouth wide open waiting to catch my load, whilst two older guys each side of him were in a similar pose, all hoping

to get lucky. This really turned me on, to think these guys were craving a taste of my load, and as the redhead and blond both said simultaneously: 'Give it to them, feed them your hot load' I just let go, and with a sigh of bliss saw my spunk, the biggest load I'd shot in weeks, shoot right into the young lad's open mouth. He closed his mouth, closed his eyes and smiled in filthy ecstasy as he swallowed the spunky mess.

I thought this was the end of the strip act, but no, as I returned to the audience, they brought other guys on stage, including the young lad who'd just eaten my cum. Lining them all up in front of the stage, they then told them to get their cocks out and start wanking. The two strippers got behind them, and working their way down from each end of the line of 10 young guys on stage, they fucked each of them in turn. As they fucked them, they brought them to climax. And as they shot, it went all over the audience. I looked around me, and the faces in the front row were all covered in cum.

Finally they got to the young lad who'd swallowed my load. The blond started jerking him off, as the redhead rammed his big cock up his arse. I moved forward, looked up and at the crucial moment opened my mouth just in time to catch a huge, sweet load of teenage cum from the lad's cock as the two strippers brought him off.

They then hauled me up on the stage again, and the two strippers ordered the young lad and myself to cuddle and kiss. 'You have exchanged spunk, you have tasted each other's loads,' said the blond stripper. 'I now pronounce you fuck/suck buddies for the rest of the night'.

To make sure we stayed together, the redhead handcuffed us together. They then hauled us off the stage and into a cubicle which had a glass window and closed circuit TV cameras. Everything the young lad and I got up to for the rest of the evening was visible to the rest of the guys in the club. We were on giant TV screens on every floor, and in every room of Fantasy Island.

But it was not just us two, other guys were let into our cubicle to do all sorts of things to us as we sucked and fucked each other. At one time the young lad was being fucked by two of us at the same time, and a cameraman actually came into the booth to get close-up shots of this, lit up by a bright light so they could see everything. Then as the young lad and I lay on the bunk doing a 69, two strapping muscle men were

fucking us both. This orgy of non-stop sex went on for two hours, till finally the two strippers came in, undid our handcuffs and released us from the Public Sex Booth as it was called.

We were both too shagged out to do much else after we were released, so we both went to get a drink in the coffee bar, and took our drinks into the cinema next door. As we went in, we were handed 3-D glasses. Settling into my seat, I enjoyed the first gay porno movie in 3-D I had ever seen. It was quite amazing; cocks stuck straight out of the screen and shot their cum straight into your face.

After about 20 minutes of this, I was getting quite horny again, and soon became aware of a very handsome guy in a suit, aged in is early 20s, who had sat down next to me and was pressing his leg up against mine. I could smell his after-shave, and I felt dizzy. Presently I felt his hand stroking my thigh, then in the darkness of the cinema he unzipped my fly and took out my cock. He started jerking me off. I reciprocated, finding his crotch and taking his long, smooth cock out. As we wanked each other in the darkness, with 3-D cocks still spunking in our faces from the screen, I felt he was near to cumming. Suddenly he let go of my cock, and fumbled in his suit pocket. He brought out a condom, and placed it over his cock. Then he whispered to me to keep jerking him off. He moaned as he reached his climax. I felt his cock jerking as he filled the condom with his spunk.

I couldn't believe what he did next. He slowly removed the spunk-filled condom, stuck his finger inside it, and then held his finger up to my mouth so I could have a taste of his load. As I tasted the sweet flavor of his thick load, I felt him slipping the spunk-filled condom over my hard cock! This was so erotic, I almost came immediately. Slowly he jerked me off with his cum-filled condom, whilst he had one arm round my neck and was French kissing me. I just felt weak as I was overcome with lust, his tongue down my throat, his after-shave filling my nostrils, and his sperm inside the condom lubricating my cock and bringing me to a tremendous climax. I shot my load into the condom, and our two orgasms mixed together.

Before I could recover, however, an old man to my left had pulled the condom off my cock, now filled with my spunk and that of the young suited-man next to me, and as we watched he held it up above his face and emptied the contents into his mouth, then licked the condom out to get the last drop of our cum cocktail. Was there no end to the depravity in this den of iniquity? The old man smiled gratefully, and thanked us for

the 'show' and for the meal, then walked off in the direction of the Lust Boxes, presumably to pay a rent boy to bring him off.

I couldn't cum any more, I'd never had so much sex in such a short space of time. I went home thoroughly exhausted, and had wet dreams for several nights afterwards.

A week later I was feeling horny again, so I paid another visit to Fantasy Island, my favorite gay sex club. This time I headed for the section marked: 'Police Station' to see what went on there.

As I walked thru the door, I could see the area was got up to look like a British police station, with policemen in full uniform standing around. Two had hold of a guy and were forcing him on to his knees. His hands were handcuffed behind his back.

'Are you thirsty?' asked a tall, dark haired policeman standing over him. Without waiting for an answer the policeman unzipped his fly and took out his big, long cock, aiming it at the guy's upturned face.

'Open yer fuckin' mouth, this nice police constable needs to have a fuckin' piss!' hissed the chunky, blond policeman holding the prisoner down on his knees.

The prisoner obediently opened his mouth, and the tall policeman started pissing right into his mouth.

'Swallow the nice hot drink PC Johnson is giving you, keep swallowing, don't you dare spill any on our nice clean floor!' said the blond policeman.

As I watched the prisoner gulping down the piss as fast as he could, I felt a hand come round from behind me and start groping me. Another policeman had come up behind me and was now unzipping my fly, and I heard him say: 'This cunt's getting turned on, Serge! Another filthy fuckin' queer we can play with.'

The policeman now had my rock hard cock out and was wanking it, whilst talking obscenities in my ear: 'Watch him drink that nice policeman's piss. Bet you wish it was your mouth being used as a policeman's urinal, don'tcha, you fuckin' faggot? Keep watching, it may be you next!'

It was all I could do to stop myself cumming as the policeman behind me jerked my cock, and I watched the blond policeman stand up in front of the prisoner and take his cock out. Soon two streams of hot police piss were streaming on to the prisoner's face and into his mouth. As some of it spilled down the prisoner's clothes and on to the floor, the tall policeman kicked the prisoner and shouted: 'I said SWALLOW! Don't fuckin' spill any!'

The poor guy on his knees swallowed twice as fast to gulp down the two streams of golden liquid, and as the first policeman finished urinating in his mouth, the blond one moved right up close and stuck his pissing cock right in the prisoner's mouth: 'Ah, what a relief! I've been holding this up all afternoon. I'm pissing right down his throat, Serge!'

Finally he finished, but neither policemen put their cocks away. Instead they started jerking off right into the guy's upturned face. First PC Johnson spunked all over the guy's face. Then the blond policeman shot his thick load right into the prisoner's open mouth.

'There, now you've been fed and had your thirst quenched! All the rules obeyed,' said the sergeant behind the counter. 'Take him to the cells, boys!'

The two policemen put their cocks away and led him to the police cells.

As I stood and watched him being led away, the police sergeant behind the counter pointed to me and said to the police constable behind me: 'Right, nick 'im!'

I was excited, but thought I'd play along with the game: 'You're arresting me? What for? I only came in to report that I'd been mugged.'

'Deserves you fuckin' right!' said the policeman behind me, as he stopped wanking me and clapped handcuffs on me. 'All queers deserve to be mugged and raped.'

The sergeant, who was only in his early 30s and had a #1 crop visible beneath his cap said: 'You're under arrest for watching an obscene act. And for exposing yourself in a police station. Take him away, police constable, he's all yours to do with as you see fit!'

I was led away into a police cell, and then I was handcuffed on my back to a lower bunk, the top one was empty. Then my legs were attached to two iron rings on the supports at the bottom end of the bunk, and the policeman sneered down at me and said: 'Know where you are, son? This is the rape cell. I'm gonna break you in for all the boys in this police station'. He then took his police truncheon off his belt, and started prodding my arse with it. He went over to a drawer, and got out a big tub of grease. Then I watched as he greased up the truncheon, then my arse. Slowly he started to ease the big truncheon into my tight hole. Slowly, slowly it entered me. It hurt at first, but gradually I got used to it.

'That's right, just learn to accept it. Take that big police truncheon, we need to open up that arse for all the police cocks you're going to get tonight. Starting with this one!' he said, as he put the truncheon down, and unzipped his fly. Out popped the biggest cock I'd ever seen in my life. It must have been 12" long and was very thick.

The red-haired policeman wasn't even gentle with this monster weapon, he just rammed it straight into my greased arse. Even though I'd been 'broken in' by the truncheon, it made me yell out and my eyes were watering as my arse was filled with his throbbing hunk of police cock.

Mercilessly he fucked me whilst shouting: 'Take that, bitch! You're my fuckin' bitch, understand! Now take it and stop whining! I'm gonna fuckin' cum right up your fuckin' pussy cunt!'

Screaming as he reached his massive orgasm, I felt his monster cock pumping what seemed like a gallon of spunk into my arse. Then as suddenly as he had rammed it in there, he took it out, spat on me and walked out of the cell. But instead of slamming the door shut, another policeman came in, and I saw there was a whole line of them waiting to rape me. In all I counted 26 policemen, all in full uniform, who fucked me one after the other. I didn't even see some of their faces.

Then the sergeant came in with a glass of steaming hot yellow liquid. Of course I knew what it was. He removed my handcuffs and leg irons and sat down next to my bunk.

'One of the police constables thought you might be thirsty, so he made you a hot drink', he said, handing me the glass of piss.

I took it nervously, and sniffed. It was definitely piss. But who's was it, I wondered?

'Don't worry about who gave it to you, just drink it!' ordered the sergeant, so I took gingerly took a sip.

'Drink it all down, and I'll tell you who was generous enough to provide you with your nightcap,' he said.

I drained the glass, and then the sergeant called out: 'Come in, PC Jenkins, he loved your piss.'

I couldn't believe my eyes when in walked none other than a very handsome famous Hollywood actor, dressed in British police uniform! He came over to my bunk and said in an excellent British accent: 'Did you enjoy the drink I gave you? Now would you like to taste my load? Millions of men and women lust for it.'

With that he sat astride my chest, took out his cock and started jerking off in my face. I could see a big glob of pre-cum on the tip, and he ordered me to stick out my tongue and taste it. I didn't need telling twice. An electric thrill ran thru me as my tongue connected with this handsome actor's pre-cum. It tasted delicious, and God, I'd just drunk a whole glass of his piss as well without even realizing it!

I nearly fainted, as he eased his cock into my mouth. 'That's right, suck my cock. You've tasted my piss and pre-cum, now you're gonna get a load of my thick, sweet sperm. Keep sucking. I'm nearly there. Here it cums!'

With that, he shot the most delicious load of thick, hot spunk in my mouth that I've ever tasted. I couldn't believe this was happening, but there was more. I suddenly realized the whole thing was being filmed for a porno movie. These were now so popular, that mainstream actors were making porno movies for showing on satellite TV. People all over the world would see me drinking this sexy heartthrob's piss and spunk. Boy, would they envy me!

As my head reeled with all the excitement, he sat down next to me, and started jerking me off saying: 'You loved the taste of my policeman's load, didn't you? Show me how much you loved drinking my cum and

piss!' Of course he brought me off in seconds, and I shot pints so hard it splattered the bottom of the bunk above.

Afterwards they took my address and promised to send me a copy of the DVD, entitled: 'Police Gang Rape' starring the Hollywood actor. They needn't have bothered, it was on some of the horny gay cable channels a few months later. I was just glad my mother and father never watched them!

I realized, when I watched the movie, that this actor was the 10th policeman who raped me whilst I was chained to the bunk. I'd been raped by so many in quick succession that I didn't even notice that one had been a man once voted the sexiest in the world!

What's more, I got to chat with this Hollywood actor afterwards. 'I'll give you my autograph, unless you'd like something else to remember me by?' he winked. I got his autograph, a bottle of his piss to keep (I saw him fill the bottle personally for me), AND I got paid generously for my part in the movie.

I keep the bottle labeled with his name in my fridge, and have a sip whenever I watch one of his movies and have a wank at the same time.

Fantasy Island really does make fantasies come true!

Weeks passed, and I hadn't been to my favorite gay club, Fantasy Island, so I decided it was high time I paid another visit.

This time, however, I noticed something different. Building work had been going on outside the club the last time I visited, but now the scaffolding had been removed I saw that a public convenience had opened right next door to the main entrance of the club. What was curious about it though was that there was only a Gents, no Ladies. Moreover, a notice outside said: 'Adults only, strictly no minors. You must be aged 18 or over. Proof of age may be requested.'

I walked in to investigate, and there was a security guard making sure no minors came in. But inside it looked like a perfectly ordinary public convenience. A few men standing at the urinals, but nothing outrageous was going on. I then decided to look in one of the cubicles lined up against the far wall. One was vacant and I went in. Unusually the toilet

basin, instead of facing you as you walked in thru the door, was affixed to the wall adjoining the next cubicle. I immediately saw why. In the wall facing the door were two little panels with knobs attached. On these panels were arrows and the words: 'Slide this way to open'.

Curious, I sat down and slid one of the little panels along to reveal a glory-hole. I peered thru, and realized I was looking into a section of the Fantasy Island gay club next door. I then slid the other panel open, and there was another glory hole. I waited a few minutes, and then someone came up to the glory hole and looked thru. He was a typical middle-aged skinhead type with a shaved head, goatee beard and little 'tache. He put his finger thru the hole, inviting me to slip my cock thru.

So this is what they had been building! A cottage where members of the general public could pop in to get a quick blow-job. I was amazed, but I declined the offer of the skinhead as he wasn't really my type, but I knew exactly where I was going to head when I got inside the club!

Having paid my entrance fee, I headed straight for where I knew the public convenience was situated. I saw a new section of the club had opened, and on the door was a notice saying this led to 'The Public Servicing Room'. I pushed the door open excitedly, and saw that there was a row of glory-holes this side leading thru to the cubicles in the men's public toilet the other side of the wall. Some of the glory-holes were occupied this side. Guys were sucking off cocks, and one was being sucked or wanked off.

I walked over to two unoccupied glory-holes. There was a bench to sit on this side, so I sat and waited with eager anticipation. The panels the other side of the wall were shut, but after about five minutes I heard noises the other side of the wall, and presently the panels were slid open. I looked thru, and what I saw took my breath away! A young policeman in full uniform was in there, and as I watched he stood up and slowly unzipped his fly. I didn't know what to do. Should I be bold and put my finger thru? I needn't have worried because a moment later his long, smooth, circumcised cock came thru the hole. I leaned forward and took a sniff of this delicious young blond policeman's meaty truncheon.

I almost fainted as I stuck out my tongue and made contact with the beautiful head, glistening with pre-cum. An electric thrill shot thru me, and then I took the whole head into my mouth. He pushed his cock

right in and down my throat, and started fucking my mouth. I couldn't believe this was happening: a real policeman was in the public toilet next door fucking my mouth thru the glory-hole! This was one of my ultimate fantasies.

As I was sucking him, feeling his cock get harder and harder in my mouth, a note was pushed thru the other glory-hole. It was obviously a sheet from the policeman's official notepad, as it was headed in blue printed letters with the words METROPOLITAN POLICE alongside their logo. Scribbled on the paper was the following message: 'You're sucking off an officer of the law, faggot! Get ready to be fed a creamy lunch of thick, sweet police constable's cum!'

I felt the young policeman's cock throb in my mouth as he neared his climax. I stared straight ahead at the dark blue serge of his trouser uniform the other side of the hole, he hadn't even pulled his trousers down, just unzipped and put his cock thru the fly and the glory-hole to be serviced by some fag. I heard him moaning softly as he started to orgasm in my mouth. Greedily I savored the sweet, thick load as it spurted into my mouth straight from this gorgeous policeman's cock. Soon I had to swallow, and swallow again. Four times I swallowed, and still my mouth was full of policeman's spunk! Another note came thru on police notepaper: 'Did you enjoy your police meal as much as I enjoyed feeding you? You fuckin' queer bastard! To help you swallow it all down here's a hot drink!'

I opened my mouth, and sure enough the policeman started to piss. Eagerly I clamped my lips over his pissing cock, and just drank and drank this policeman's urine as he relieved himself down my throat. This was sheer depravity and filth, but it tasted delicious, and I felt faint as he finally withdrew his cock, and pushed thru a final note on police notepaper: 'Your mouth is just a police cum-bag and a police urinal! All queers should be forced to drink police cum and piss every day! I enjoyed feeding you. Be here this time next week for another meal and a hot drink.'

I was so worked up, I almost came without even touching my cock. But 5 minutes later the panels were opened again, and this time I saw a young office worker in a smart suit, collar and tie. He must have popped in during his lunch-hour. I poked my finger thru the glory-hole, then looked thru and saw him give me a filthy, dirty, lust-filled smile. He unzipped and came closer to the glory-hole. I could smell his overpowering aftershave as he slowly put his big prick thru the hole. He

must have drenched his cock in aftershave, as the smell was so strong, and I could taste it as I took it into my mouth.

Five minutes later I'd been fed another load of thick, sweet spunk. I swallowed it down, as he zipped up and went out. Immediately someone else came in. The office worker had left the glory-hole panels open, so I could see that this time it was the young guy from the snack-bar over the road. He was in his early twenties, with curly black hair, and wore the tightest white t-shirt which revealed all his muscles. I had often gone in for a coffee or a sandwich just to be served by this Adonis and ogle him, but he couldn't be gay surely? His girlfriend worked with him in the snack-bar, and I'd caught them kissing and cuddling at times when the snack-bar was nearly empty. But why would he use this public toilet?

There was one in the snack bar for the staff. It was lunch-time, their busiest period, so he must have left his girlfriend doing all the work whilst he popped across the road to be serviced!

I didn't need asking, I just put my mouth straight up to the glory-hole and a moment later his big cock filled my mouth. He pumped and pumped furiously, then let out a sigh as he shot 6 big wads of spunk right down my throat. My mouth was overflowing with his delicious cum. He'd reached a climax in less than a minute, and then he'd zipped up and was gone back over the road before his girlfriend hardly even missed him!

You didn't normally get these 'straight' types in a gay club. In fact none of these three I'd just sucked off would have entered a gay club, I was pretty sure of that. What a brilliant idea to make a public toilet with glory-holes leading into a gay club, so those bisexual and closet gays who wouldn't be seen dead going into a gay club could get in on the action. I'd heard of public toilets with big glory-holes in the bad old days before clubs with gay backrooms opened, but now they were all gone.

Most public conveniences had been closed for lack of money to keep them open, or replaced by horrible, coin-in-the-slot unisex French-style toilet booths. Any still left had the glory-holes blocked up.

Now I saw the excitement of 'public cottage glory-holes'. You literally didn't know who would come in next. There was a barracks down the road; maybe I'd get a soldier in uniform sooner or later? But not today, I'd been very lucky as it was.

However, someone else did come in. A cute looking guy with long blond hair down to his neck. He had pouting rosy lips; so pretty that he almost looked like a girl! He had a thin gold chain around his neck, and a red t-shirt on. I guess he was about 18 or 19. He knelt by the hole and pressed his lips up close to the glory-hole. I heard him whisper: 'Feed me, feed me, please feed me!' I was so worked up by now, my cock was rock hard. I pushed it thru the glory-hole into his rose-bud lips, which immediately started to suck me dry. I was in heaven, this was bliss! A beautiful teenage boy was sucking me off. I couldn't hold out any longer. With a scream of ecstasy I let go about 7 big spurts of spunk right into his sucking mouth. It felt so good; I was feeding him like a baby! I looked thru as I zipped up, and he was gurgling with delight, my cum all over his lips. He stood up and put his lovely cock thru, and I just had to return the favor. I sucked it and a few minutes later was rewarded with the sweetest load of cum I'd had in a long time.

I left the club fully satisfied, determined to go back again the very next day for more of this servicing the public!

BEGGING FOR IT

My boss and master was always thinking up new ways to humiliate me. Making me beg for all my meals, from breakfast to dinner, which always began with a big mouthful of hot spunk from his cock. Then he'd bring his friends around to feed me their loads as well.

For my 19th birthday he bought me a whole load of t-shirts which he told me I had to wear whenever he took me out anywhere. The red one with yellow lettering he ordered me to wear today read: 'I'm A Cum Eater. Please feed me'.

I had got a job as an office boy just last year, and he had trained me to sit under his desk and suck him off whilst he interviewed clients and prospective employees. Several months after I started working there, he took me home with him and told me that's where I'd be living from now on. He made me write a letter to my parents saying I'd be living with my boss from now on.

Today we had to go into work as usual, but he said as it was my birthday we could both go in late, as he had some birthday treats lined up for me in the morning.

Wearing the t-shirt as we left the apartment, I felt very conspicuous and humiliated already as people looked at me with disgust. Teenagers were openly pointing and laughing at me, even shouting obscenities. A gang of young skinheads saw my t-shirt and started groping their cocks and shouting: 'I've got a big load for yer!', 'Wanna suck my cock, queerboy?', etc.

'Look, those nice boys want to give you some birthday presents. Go up to them and ask for their loads,' said my master.

He pushed me towards the group. 'Hi guys!,' he said. 'This faggot wants to ask you something. It's his birthday today. Go on, Cumslut, ask these nice lads for your presents!'

I looked at the 6 strapping young skinheads in their Ben Sherman shirts, braces, jeans and bovver boots, and my cock grew rock hard.

'My mouth is at your service, please feed me your spunky loads' I said. 'My mouth is watering to taste your young tasty skinhead orgasms!'

They laughed and sneered, then led me into an alleyway. My master followed.

'On your knees, these nice lads are going to feed you!' he said.

I fell to me knees and the leader of the group, a tall, muscular skin, unzipped his jeans and took out a huge 10" monster. 'Suck on this, faggot!' he said,. I did as he ordered me, and the 5 other skins stood around and took their cocks out too. I was surrounded by big skinhead cocks, and had to suck them all in quick succession as they jerked themselves close to climax.

'OK, here it cums, breakfast time, cunt-face!' said the leading skinhead. I opened my mouth wide and he shoved his big cock inside and pumped my mouth and throat full to overflowing with his thick, hot load.

Before I could swallow it, another skinhead was cumming all over my face.

I opened my mouth again and his second, third and fourth spurts shot into my mouth, mixing with the spunk of the first skinhead. One by one all six of them unloaded their spunky cocks into my mouth. Their

skinhead loads tasted delicious, and I swallowed their big cummy cocktail eagerly, and got shakily to my feet as they walked away, zipping themselves up and laughing.

With skinhead spunk all over my face and chin, and over my t-shirt, my master took me out of the alleyway, and almost immediately we saw two young policemen in their traditional British helmets, dark blue trousers and lighter blue short-sleeved shirts showing off their sexy arms and biceps.

'Go on, ask these nice policemen to feed you,' ordered my master.

They had already seen the disgusting state I was in, and read the obscene message on my t-shirt, so when I approached them and spoke they were already looking at me with contempt.

'Please may I drink your police spunk? My mouth is at your service, officers!' I said.

'You disgusting little pervert!' said the tall blond policeman.

'Let's feed the fucker in that doorway,' said his dark-haired fellow officer. 'I'm horny as Hell, I could do with a good teenage mouth to give me some relief.'

The two policemen pushed me into the doorway of a shop which wasn't yet open, unzipped their flies and both shoved their big police 'truncheons' into my mouth at the same time.

'Here, suck some police cock!' said the blond police officer.

'Do it good, remember you're sucking officers of the law!' sneered the other one.

They made groaning noises as they both neared their climax, then the blond one shouted: 'Oh, yeah, I'm cummin'! I'm gonna feed him a huge load of police sperm! Taste this spunky mess!' With that he pumped my mouth and throat full of his thick, hot police semen. It tasted really sweet, and as I moaned and started to swallow it, the dark-haired policeman shoved his cock back into my spunky mouth: 'God, that looks so obscene! It's brought me off. Now taste my orgasm, you queer

bastard! Aaarggh! Oh, oh! oh!' he groaned in ecstasy as he unloaded into my willing mouth. 'How do you like the flavor of MY police sperm?'

I swallowed their loads, and said: 'I love the taste of your sperm, sir! Both of you have delicious spunk. Thank you for feeding it to me.'

'So you love the taste of police spunk, do you?' said the blond policeman, coming up behind me and putting his smooth, sexy arm over my face so my nose and mouth were buried in his bicep. The clean soapy policeman smell almost made me faint, and with his other strong arm he was groping my hard cock. I almost came in my pants as I involuntarily stuck out my tongue and started licking the policeman's bicep. It tasted as delicious as he smelt!

'He's still begging for it,' said the blond policeman, turning to my master. 'Bring him to the police station tonight. We'll keep him in the cells overnite and all 50 police constables will feed him their loads, and fuck the shit out of him'.

My master promised to deliver me to the police to be used as their cum dump, then dragged me out of the shop doorway and down the Tube.

On the platform was a young office executive with red hair, dressed in a smart gray suit with a laptop under his arm.

'Go up to that man and ask to drink his spunk' ordered my master.

I knew the drill. On the crowded platform I went up to him and said: 'Please, sir, I bet your cum tastes lovely. I'd love to drink it. Please feed me your sperm, sir!'

The young man looked shocked and surprised, and several other passengers overheard and looked at me in disgust and disbelief.

'Please, please feed me your spunk, sir! I'm so hungry, I haven't been fed any sperm for 5 minutes' I whimpered. People moved away in embarrassment, but not the young man. I could see his cock swelling with anticipation in his suit trousers. This man smelt good; he was wearing my favorite after-shave, Tommy Hilfiger, which makes any young man quite irresistible. Any young man wearing Tommy Hilfiger just has to be sucked off and given a tongue-bath. That is why they

wear it, because they know their spunk and smooth, sexy bodies are irresistible to sluts like me when they wear that seductive fragrance.

The young executive caught me sniffing, and said: 'You like my Tommy fragrance, do you? It's a new version called "Suck Me". And you want me to feed you? Come with me.' With my master following, the young man led me thru a passage-way and into a corridor where there was an emergency spiral staircase leading up to the street. He shoved me down on my knees, stood up on the second step and unzipped. The smell of Tommy Hilfiger 'Suck Me' fragrance overwhelmed me as I looked at the smooth, circumcised young executive cock sticking obscenely out of his gray suit trousers, the head glistening with a big glob of pre-cum. I stuck my tongue out and a filthy electric thrill shot thru me as I tasted his delicious juices.

'That's right, lick up my pre-cum. It'll serve as a taster for the main course,' said the young executive, as he fucked my mouth. The taste of his sweet pre-cum mixed with the taste and overwhelming smell of his Tommy 'Suck Me' fragrance made me dizzy as I looked up into his face contorted with pure lust as he neared his climax.

'Oh yeah! Drink my load of baby-making juice!' he said, as he shot spurt after spurt of the most delicious tasting spunk I'd ever tasted into my mouth and down my throat. As he was feeding me, four sixth-form college boys came down the spiral staircase dressed in their smart college maroon blazers, gray trousers, white shirts and gray ties. They were all aged about 18 to 20. They saw what was happening, and started laughing and getting their own cocks out to be sucked off.

'Look, a queer is sucking guys off in the Underground!' said the blond-haired college boy. 'Let's get in on the action!'

'Ask them nicely,' ordered my master.

As the young executive zipped up, picked up his lap-top and walked away with a satisfied smile on his face, I looked up at the four handsome young college lads in their smart uniforms and said: 'I'm so hungry for your teenage spunk. Please may I taste your college boy loads? Please, please feed me!'

The slightly older blond one was wearing a. badge marked 'Prefect'. He came up to me and slowly unzipped his trousers, taking out his long, uncut cock.

'Yeah, we'll feed you plenty of college boy spunk! Taste my Prefect's load first. All younger boys at college drink it regularly, they have to. It's part of a Prefect's perks to get sucked off by new 18 year old college freshers. This is what you're missing, a tasty college boy cock filled with delicious Prefect's sperm ready to explode into your mouth,' he said as he slowly pushed his lovely cock into my mouth and down my throat.

I sucked and sucked, tasting his delicious college boy cock, and the other college boys stood round jerking their cocks waiting to feed me their loads too. This was so obscene, a fantasy come true. I'd missed out on all this fun at my own college, where nothing like this ever happened. Now I could feel the blond Prefect's cock trembling in my mouth as it grew rock hard and started to spew hot, sweet college-boy sperm into my mouth and down my throat.

'Yeah, oh yeah! Drink my spunky load, drink my Prefect's milk, it's good for growing boys!' said the blond Prefect. 'Feed him, boys, feed him your college-boy loads now!'

The other college boys did as their Prefect ordered, and in quick succession I was fed mouthfuls of a red-headed college-boy's cum, another load from a dark haired one with a gorgeous golden tan. His spunk tasted the best of all and I actually came in my pants as I tasted it.

But I still had to drink the load of the last college boy, with a fair #1 crop and cold blue eyes. His cock was 12" long and went straight down my throat, choking me. His spunky orgasm filled my throat and overflowed into my mouth, making me gag.

'Drink it, cock-sucker!' barked the college boy, as he continued to pump his huge load out of his monster cock straight down my throat and into my spunk-swelled belly.

After I'd been fed by the four college boys, my master took me on to a Tube train and into work. But not before I'd been forced to suck off another office executive, this one in a smart black suit. I had to whisper in his ear: 'May I drink your orgasm, sir?' Then sink to my knees and

suck him off in the rush-hour crowd. Nobody noticed as he fed me his delicious cream in the crowded Tube train, nor as I stood up, looked straight into his handsome face with his spunk in my mouth and over my lips, licked them clean and whispered: 'Thank you for your thick cream, sir!' and swallowed the lot. He gave me his business card and whispered: 'Come to my office tomorrow and service me and my young executives!'

'See what you get, if you ask nicely?' said my master. He took me into work, where as usual I had to service him and all the young male office workers in their smart shirts and suits, sitting under their desks and sucking them all off one by one. I drank another 56 loads of spunk in the office that day.

In the evening my boss and master took me to a public toilet and made me suck off another 58 men thru a glory-hole into the next cubicle, whilst he sat on the toilet seat next to me and spoke obscenities in my ear, and from time to time jerked me off saying things like: 'Drink that sperm!', 'You like the taste of that load, don't you?', 'How do you like the flavour of that orgasm?', 'He's giving you your birthday boy cream. Thank him for his sperm', etc..

I put my mouth to the glory hole and thanked the last man for his spunky load. I hadn't seen what he and half the other men even looked like, but my heart missed a beat as I saw I had just sucked off my own older brother! A very handsome married man with two young kids, I never knew he did things like this in public toilets. I'd lusted after him secretly since we reached adolescence.

'Happy birthday, little brother!' he said as he recognized me. 'I'll have to feed you my load more often. You're a great cock-sucker. Be here tomorrow same time!'

Brothers and other young men are so nice to sluts like me. They are only to willing to feed a spunk-hungry mouth like mine.

After this, I was delivered to the police station by my master, where I spent the whole night satisfying all the policemen in the station by drinking loads of police sperm. I've to go back next week; they're bringing in colleagues from another police station so I've got some new flavors next time. Also some soldiers from the nearby barracks have been invited along to be serviced in their uniforms.

If I do my job well, I'll be hired out by my master to all the police stations and barracks in the area. It's all go for a cock-sucker slut like me!

GLOSSARY OF BRITISH WORDS, TERMS AND SLANG USED IN THIS BOOK

allotment	plot of land for growing vegetables, etc. hired out to city dwellers on available land, often next to railroad tracks
Anderson shelter	Wartime air-raid shelter half buried in people's back gardens or backyards
arse	ass (posterior, not a donkey)
barrage balloons	huge balloons floated above crucial sites to make bombing from the air difficult
biscuit	cookie

blackout	Wartime regulations which banned all visible lights outside after dark to make air bombing more difficult
block of flats	apartment block
bollock naked	stark naked or completely naked (bollocks being slang for a man's private parts)
bovver boots	literally 'bother boots' - Doc Martin boots worn by skinheads (who like giving people a lot of 'aggro' or 'bovver')
boys in blue	policemen
braces	suspenders
Brylcreem	greasy hairdressing popular in earlier decades
bumhole	asshole
call-up/called-up	a reference to the draft into military service (ended in early 1960s, also called National Service)
Chelsea Pensioner	senior citizen war veteran in distinctive uniform of Royal Hospital, Chelsea, London
cocky	sassy
conscription	a reference to the draft into military service
cottages	gay slang for a public restroom
cottaging	cruising public restrooms for gay sex
Cumminal	made-up word based on 'urinal' describing an imaginery jerk-off/suck off booth
dahn	down (Cockney pronunciation)

dong	a slang word for 'cock'
Freedom Pass	senior citizen's/disabled person's pass given free travel on much public transport
French Letter	slang for a condom
fresher	a first year student at college or university
gob	slang for 'mouth'
gobbed	spat
Heath-Robinson	cartoonist who depicted crazy, impractical inventions and pieces of machinery
jelly	jello
land-girls	women volunteers working on farms during WWII
lawyer	attorney
lost his marbles	lost his wits, or went a bit crazy
mate/matey	friend/friendly
milk monitors	in 30 years or so after WWII school/college students were given free milk twice a day, sometimes handed out by students called 'milk monitors'
mincemeat	also shredded meat (as well as US meaning of sweet currant-based pie filling)
Morrison shelter	Wartime internal shelter constructed under a table to protect people if the house collapsed on top of them
mum	mom

nick 'im/nick him	arrest him
Nissan hut	hut, usually military, made of curved corrugated iron
old lag	convict serving a long-term prison sentence
pants	briefs or underpants (not trousers in UK)
petrol	gasoline
posh	classy (from old-fashioned cruising acronym P.O.S.H. for 1st class passenger cabins location: Port Outward, Starboard Home)
prefect	like a monitor, a student given authority over other students
Private/Pvte	lowest rank in British army
public convenience	public restroom
public toilet	public restroom
punk	another British/European teenage tribe into piercings, anarchism, etc.
RAF	Royal Air Force
railway lines	railroad tracks
randy	horny
Redcaps	British Military Police
scally boys	working class youths wearing baseball caps, tracksuits and other sportswear

second floor	third floor (in Britain the first floor is known as the ground floor, the second floor as the first floor, etc.)
skinheads/skins	tribe of youths wearing Doc Martin boots, Ben Sherman shirts, tight jeans with suspenders. They have shaved heads.
slapper	a woman of easy virtue, also known as a slag or a slut
sod	literally short for 'sodomite', but used as a mild insult
Spunkinal	made-up word based on 'urinal' describing an imaginary jerk-off/suck off booth
squaddies	ordinary British soldiers
snog/snogging	passionate sexual kiss/kissing
shag/shagging	fuck/fucking
shortbread finger	shortbread cookie (elongated rectangular shape)
sixth-former	high school students in their last year (16 years old or more)
spunk	also means 'cum' in Britain
spunky	covered in cum, full of cum or pertaining to cum
tap	faucet
Tardis/Dr Who	Refers to time machine and popular long-running sci-fi BBC TV series 'Dr Who'. Tardis looks like police phone booth outside, but is much bigger inside

tenner	a ten pound note (currency bill)
throw the book at	come down with full weight of the law or regulations
throw up	be sick/to vomit
truncheon	police baton
Tube	London's subway railroad system (to be precise, the deep-level part of the system)
Underground	London's subway railroad system
wank	jerk off/masturbate
wanking	jerking off

ABOUT THE AUTHOR

Ted Gay has had erotic gay fantasies published on various gay Internet sites, but this is the first time some of his stories have been collected together and published in book format. Ted was born and still lives in London, England, and under another name wrote a regular column for a music magazine, and has had numerous articles on various subjects published, including one in 1991 calling for a liberalization of Britain's restrictive laws on homosexuality. A decade later, backroom clubs, gay saunas, etc. became legal in the United Kingdom for the first time.

www.ingramcontent.com/pod-product-compliance
Lightning Source LLC
Chambersburg PA
CBHW051142260626
47170CB00005B/1928